I don't *need* ch
right now I'm weak.

Leaving the box sealed, I reach through the broken window and pull out an individually wrapped cupcake. I shouldn't be tempted. My stomach is full of good food—a delicately seasoned chicken breast, strawberries, walnuts and greens drizzled with light poppy-seed dressing. None of that is junk.

This is.

My hand closes around the wrapper. I should crush it… the way I crushed that whole display in Smiley's. Instead I pop it open.

I have to know. I have to know why Rob couldn't stop eating these things.

My hand is shaking as I lift the cupcake toward my mouth. The frosting oozes across my tongue now, melting. The cake is sweet and moist. The frosting is dark and bitter. The filling is creamy and sweet. The combination is euphoric.

And now I understand Rob.

Lisa Childs

Award-winning author **Lisa Childs** wrote her first book, a biography...of the family dog, when she was six. Now she writes romantic suspense and women's fiction. The youngest of seven siblings, she holds family very dear, in real life and in her fiction, often infusing her books with compelling family dynamics. She lives in west Michigan with her husband, two daughters and a twenty-pound Siamese cat. For the latest on Lisa's spine-tingling suspense and heartwarming women's fiction, check out her Web site at www.lisachilds.com. She loves hearing from readers, who can also reach her at P.O. Box 139, Marne, MI 49435.

Lisa Childs

Learning to Hula

LEARNING TO HULA

copyright © 2006 by Lisa Childs-Theeuwes

isbn-13:9780373881055

isbn-10:   0373881053

TheNextNovel.com

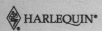 HARLEQUIN®

PRINTED IN U.S.A.

From the Author

Dear Reader,

One of my best friends is a widow, twice. I have always marveled at how strong this little, four-foot-nine, ninety-pound woman is to have survived losing not only one love of her life, but two. And she hasn't just survived— she's happy again.

I've wondered how I would handle such an unspeakable tragedy, to lose the man I love. My husband is one of those fun-loving, never-met-a-stranger types who makes me laugh every day. How would I laugh without him? Like the main character in *Learning To Hula*, I'm sure I'd focus on my children and lean on my family while I passed through all the stages of grief and, like Holly, I'd learn to hula and find happiness again. Being strong is more a state of mind than body.

Wishing you every happiness!

Lisa Childs

To: Tara Gavin, with deep appreciation, for your vision
and dedication to Harlequin NEXT. Thank you for
including my stories in this empowering, relevant series.
Jennifer Green, with special thanks, for your insight
and guidance. I love working with you!
Jenny Bent, my amazing agent, thank you for your
constant encouragement and unwavering support!
Mary Gardner, for always being a true friend.

PROLOGUE

The experts say that when you suffer a loss, you pass through five stages of grief: denial, anger, bargaining, depression and acceptance.

Well, I'm certainly no expert despite all the experience I've been getting lately. But I think there are more than five. Or maybe I only think that because I've been through each stage so many times that I've stopped labeling them.

At any rate I know which stage the experts have omitted. Happiness. And I know you can find that stage again no matter what kind of loss you've suffered....

STAGE 1

Holly DeJong. That's the name on the check. Not the signature, but on the payable-to line, which is good since that's my name, and there are a lot of zeroes in the box after it.

A lot of zeroes but still not the most I've seen. I got a bigger check six months ago…when I buried my husband.

"Do you have any questions?" the bank manager asks.

I shake my head. My hand is shaking, too, as I pick up the pen I just used to sign all the documents; I endorse the back of the check and hand it to him. "Here, you take it."

"Holly…"

"Do your magic with it, Keith," I tell him. I'd given him the other check, too, and already the account he put it in has added zeroes to the original total.

Rob would like that, that the value of his life has kept increasing even after his death. That's what that first check represented—his life. The second, for the sale of his business, represents his life's work.

I know he would make some joke about all the zeroes; he was always making jokes. Sometimes I think he's not really dead, just pulling one of his pranks that usually amused only him, and taking it too far.

"Holly, are you sure?" Keith asks.

I glance up from the check and focus on him, staring at his dark suit and the matching circles beneath his eyes. His hair, once dark, too, has gone mostly gray. He hasn't looked this old in all the years I've known him.

And I've known him a long time, ever since he started dating my oldest sister, Pam. He's been married to her for twenty-five years.

But if she has her way, they won't make twenty-six. She's left him. I'm not sure which has made him look old so suddenly, twenty-five years of marriage to her finally catching up with him, or her leaving.

The latter is why he's hesitating to take the check, why he hesitated to participate in the closing to begin with. But the twenty-five year relationship is why I would trust no one else.

For the past six months he's held my hand and guided me through the maze of paperwork involved with settling an estate and transferring ownership of a business.

"Keith, you're always going to be my brother."

I have none, just two sisters. Emma, the second oldest one, has been married twice, but I never felt as close to either of her husbands as I have to Keith. I can't understand why Pam is leaving him.

She blames Rob.

She blamed him for a lot of things when he was alive; I shouldn't have expected his death to change that. Pam never understood his sense of humor, so the only thing she "got" about the practical jokes he played on her was angry. After he let the air out of her tires once, she blamed him every time she got a flat, and whenever something sticky was on her door handle, she thought Rob was fooling around with the peanut butter again.

Despite their mutual antagonism, she claims that his death somehow brought her clarity. She can't put off doing what she really wants because she sees now that life is too short.

They hadn't agreed on much when he was alive, but Rob wouldn't be able to argue that one with her. He'd been forty-one when he died.

Death by cupcake is what I call it. He lied and cheated on me with those things, breaking every promise he made to cut them out of his life and stick to the diet I put him on. I should have known he was lying. A man's waistband doesn't keep expanding like that. He'd called it a beer belly, but he'd never been able to swallow a sip of beer; he'd hated the taste of it. He actually hadn't liked anything that wasn't sweet.

Well, at least Pam got something out of his death. I got nothing but zeroes. Lots of them, thanks to all the life insurance Rob had bought from one of his clients, an insurance agent. When he'd made the purchases, I'd thought it sweet of him to support the man's business. I hadn't realized it would one day be supporting us.

Before Keith can overcome the emotion I see in his watery eyes, and say anything about my loyalty to him, the buyers come back into his office. They just rushed out a little while ago, buoyant with the pride and excitement of ownership.

These are the kids who worked for Rob, who helped him build his computer business. I'm glad they bought it. They're Rob's second choice to take over, but I can't hang on to the store until our son grows up. Robbie's only fifteen, and I can't presume that his father's dream will be his, even though my son says it is. I want him and his eleven-year-old sister, Claire, to first get through this nightmare of losing their father, then come up with and realize their own dreams.

Just as Brad, Jake and Steven realized theirs, of owning their own business. The three of them are in their early twenties and they look more like surfers, with their long, shaggy hair and baggy clothes, than computer geeks. But they have enough computer savvy and experience for Keith to give them a business loan.

Jake and Steven walk toward me, holding a big cardboard box. The money is enough; I hope they haven't brought me anything else.

"You missed this stuff when you cleaned out Rob's office," Brad says. He'll be the manager, as he's the one who usually talks for the three of them. He's the one who asked if I'd sell to them. Although they would never admit it, their decision to buy was probably as much to get me out of the office as to own the business themselves. I worked there before Rob died, *for* him, *with* them; it was different after.

Everything is.

"So what's in the box?" Not that I can't guess.

More cupcakes. I found them stashed everywhere after his death—in the desk in his den, his sock drawer, car console and tackle box. I really should have had a clue, other than his growing belly, of what Rob had been doing. The man had never gone fishing a day in his life.

Predictably Brad lifts out a box of the decadent cupcakes. The guys are laughing. Rob had probably thought it was freaking funny, too.

A big joke on me.

Who's having the last laugh now? I'd like to know. I haven't laughed much since he died. I force a smile and knot my hands in my lap to still their trembling. It's not nerves.

Nothing that simple.

I'm boomeranging back to stage two again. Anger.

I can feel it building, but I fight it. I'm past it. I've done all the five stages of grief. I've even managed stage five, acceptance, or I wouldn't have sold the business.

I'm doing great. Just like my mom did when my dad died six years ago. She's my little five-foot, hundred-pound how-to guide on being a widow. She handled it. So can I.

Brad pulls something else out of the box, slowly so that at first all I see is the grass-covered shade, then the rest of the lamp follows. Silken black hair spills over his fingers and coconut-covered breasts peek out from between them. The grass skirt rustles against the box as he lifts the object free and settles it on Keith's desk.

The shade swings around as the hula girl base wobbles back and forth. Dangerous. That's what it is. A fire hazard. I'd told Rob that he needed to get rid of it, and he'd promised he had—apparently another lie.

The guys are laughing, and even Keith has a smile on his face, something I haven't seen since Pam moved out of their house. "That's so Rob," he sputters, and there's more emotion in his eyes than humor. The two men were close.

"It's tacky," I manage to say around the emotion clogging my throat.

Through the windows of Keith's office, I spy other customers stopping to stare at the hideous thing. I should be embarrassed. Stanville, Michigan, is a small town; probably most of those people know me. But after being married to Rob for seventeen years, I'm beyond embarrassment.

He once dressed up like a hula girl for Halloween, using the same excuse for his costume as he had for his purchase of the lamp—it reminded him of our Hawaiian honeymoon.

Now, staring at the lamp, I'm reminded of Rob in that coconut bra with his stomach spilling over the top of his grass skirt, his black wig flowing around his broad shoulders as he swayed back and forth like the bobbing lamp.

Now I'm laughing with Keith and the guys.

Staring at the wine bottles in Smiley's store, I consider giving Pam the lamp as a housewarming gift instead. I've already been to all the other sections of Smiley's General Store, and *general* covers a lot: groceries, clothing, housewares, hardware and party supplies. Yet I haven't found a single appropriate thing for tonight.

I might as well go with inappropriate.

The truth is that I don't really feel like giving her a gift at all, but she's throwing herself a party.

Maybe bringing alcohol is a good idea. Even though she'll use it to toast her new life, *I* get to drink it, too. I suspect I'm going to need it.

So now I switch from trying to figure out what she'd

like. Keith hadn't managed that in twenty-five years, so I'm not going to figure it out in twenty minutes. I concentrate on finding my favorite labels.

Whenever he worked late, Rob would bring home a bottle of Lambrusco to mellow me. I should have realized, it's probably the sweetest wine available. Despite claiming it was for me, he'd drink most of it.

I'd always ask him, "Is this for *me?*"

He'd grin and reply, "Yes, I'm going to get you drunk so I can have my way with you."

I'd laugh and point out that he'd never had to get me drunk for that.

My hand's shaking as I reach for a bottle of Lambrusco. All this shaking today. Maybe it has nothing to do with the closing or stages, maybe I just had too much caffeine this morning. But then I remember that I drink decaf. Unlike Rob, I don't cheat on my health.

My fingers miss the bottle; I'm not tall enough, and that irritates me. Claire is already taller than I am. I take after my petite mother in more than widowhood.

Off balance from the reach, I stumble back a few steps. My hip brushes against the display behind me, tumbling some cardboard boxes onto Smiley's freshly waxed vinyl floor. I spin around to catch more before I cause an avalanche.

Startled, I see what's in my hands—familiar boxes that I've found stashed all over the house and Rob's office. The bright yellow packaging has a cellophane window in the middle displaying the heavily frosted, buttercream-filled cupcakes in their individual packages. Above the window, a little black kitten sits in the corner of the box, licking frosting from its whiskers. These are Kitty Cupcakes.

More like *killer* Kitty Cupcakes.

This time the anger rushes in so fast I can't stop it. It roars in my ears and burns my face. My hands aren't shaking anymore as I toss the boxes onto the floor.

Kitty's staring up at me with her green eyes as I lift my foot and smash my heel right through the cellophane window. Frosting and bits of chocolate cake cling to my shoe as I lift it, then slam it down again into another box. I spread my arms, toppling the entire display and standing in the middle of it, jumping up and down as if I'm having one of the tantrums my daughter, Claire, used to throw when she was two.

Words are tumbling from my lips, but I can't hear them. But they, and my actions, are drawing other shoppers to the end of the aisle.

Even though I can't hear myself, I catch a little girl's horrified whisper to her mother: "Mommy, why is that woman killing Kitty?"

The mother covers the child's eyes as if they've stumbled into a strip joint. I'm not naked, but suddenly I feel that way.

The anger ebbs. I move to step away from the pile of crumpled boxes, but my heel slips, either on the waxed floor or the spilled frosting, and I go down.

The small crowd at the end of the aisle murmurs "Ahh!" I try to scramble up, but go down again to their "Ohhs."

Frosting coats my fingers, and I glance down at the smart little suit I wore to the closing. Brown frosting clings to the black-and-white-houndstooth print like mud kicked up from the tires of a stuck truck.

I'm sure there's some in my hair, too, since locks of it are sticking to my face. I push it back, forgetting my hands are coated, and leave more frosting across my cheek.

Even though the crowd is quiet, I can hear laughter. Maybe it's coming from above; Rob would *love* this. Or maybe it's bubbling up inside me. Either way, it feels good and I start smiling, probably looking like even more of a lunatic to the spectators gathered like gawkers at a traffic accident.

Someone gets brave enough to approach me, and extend a hand to help me up. I reach for it with my sticky fingers and glance up with an apologetic grimace.

A face similar to mine stares down at me, blue eyes as wide and horrified as those of the little girl who watched me kill Kitty. Emma's fair skin tinted with the red blush of embarrassment, not for herself.

Before she can do more than get me to my feet, Smiley rushes up, rubber-soled shoes squeaking against the vinyl tiles. White brows lift high above his sharp eyes as he takes in the cupcake massacre. He asks the question burning in my sister's blue eyes. "What the hell happened here?"

Emma's faster on her feet than I am at the moment. Must be from dealing with all the teenagers she has, her own and step. "Smiley, don't worry. I'll take care of it." She's already drawing her wallet from her purse.

As Claire has done to me so many times, I tug on Emma's sleeve, and point to the alcohol wall. "Get a bottle of Lambrusco, too. I couldn't reach it."

Then I walk away, head high, frosting-covered heels slipping. The shocked crowd parts as I near the end of the party aisle and walk out of Smiley's.

STAGE 2

As I shut off the water and step from the shower, I hear voices through the door. "I don't understand what happened. She's been doing great."

This is Pam, completely puzzled by the fact that I might miss my husband. She's actually having a party over leaving hers. I wince at my cattiness. I'm not being fair. She's been there for me, offering her love and support in myriad ways. And her opinion.

Pam has an opinion about everything. If I had let her win the suit argument, Rob would be haunting me more than he already does. I can still see her mouth screwed up tightly with disapproval over my choice of Hawaiian shirt and Bermuda shorts for Rob's funeral garb. I truly believe I saw him smirking at her from the casket, glib with victory in yet another one of their disagreements.

With a steady hand, I wipe the fog from the bathroom mirror and inspect my reflection. My hair is plastered to my head. Wet, it's dark brown; dry, it's golden.

I push it behind my ears, checking for frosting back there. The ends drip water onto my shoulders and the towel I've wrapped around myself.

My suit lies in a corner of the tiny room, balled up in disgrace. I, curiously enough, feel none.

Knuckles brush softly against the other side of the door, its white paint peeling due to moisture in the unvented room.

"Are you okay?" Emma asks, her voice low with concern. The knob turns, and she opens the door, unwilling to wait for or untrusting of my response.

"I'm fine," I assure her.

She studies my face with much more scrutiny than I'd given it in the now refogged mirror. Then she hands me one of Pam's velour track suits. We're at her new place, the cramped apartment above The Tearoom, the shop my mother owns less than a block from Smiley's, in the heart of our small town.

Emma and I have houses on what's left of our dad's old dairy farm a few miles outside of town. Mom sold off most of the property after he died, dividing among the three of us what land was left and some of the money she made. The rest she used to buy this building and a condo. Pam has a house with Keith near mine and Emma's. It's a gorgeous modern contemporary with granite and slate and smooth white walls. Nothing like this place, with its exposed brick and dark wood.

I wonder again how she'll be happy here *without* Keith. She says she's leaving him because she was never happy *with* him. This is another rare thing Rob would have agreed with her on; he used to say Pam didn't know *how* to be happy.

But she does know how to shop. My fingers sink into the velour as I take the pale yellow suit from Emma. "Thanks. I'll get dressed and be right out."

She looks at me as if she wants to stay, maybe help me dress as though I'm a small, clumsy child. But she's raised three of her own and two of somebody else's; she knows when to help and when to step back and let someone go. Although she'll stop them from making dangerous decisions, she always says that kids have to make their own mistakes to grow. She leaves and shuts the door for me.

Yellow isn't a color I usually wear, but at the moment I can't be picky. Outside the bathroom, my sisters have lowered their voices to whispers. I can't hear their words, only their hushed murmuring. It takes me back to when we were younger, Emma and Pam sharing all their scandalous secrets and leaving me out.

At thirty-eight, I'm six years younger than Emma, nine younger than Pam. Back then those years had made a difference, had made me the baby, but age hasn't mattered for a long time. With Rob gone, I'm not anyone's baby anymore.

In case there are other guests, I raid Pam's medicine cabinet for powder and mascara so I look passably decent. Then I rescue my underwear from the frosted suit, hurrying to dress. I fling open the door, cutting my sisters off midwhisper as they hunch over the tiny table in Pam's kitchen. It's only the two of them, no one else.

"I hope you haven't canceled the party," I say to Pam, bracing myself to face her. I expect that same tight expression of disapproval she wore over Rob's funeral attire. Instead she's wide-eyed with concern, the way Emma looked in Smiley's when she helped me up.

I don't like that any more than the pitying glances I get from people since Rob died. "The poor widow." If they only knew how many zeroes Keith had to work with.

Pam shakes her head, then runs her fingers through her new short bob. "No. This is it. Just us."

No other friends? But then the three of us are so close, we are as much or more friends than sisters.

I smile at her, hoping to reassure her. Then I gesture toward the stained butcher-block counter where the Lambrusco sits. "Nobody's opened the wine?"

Three short strides bring me to the counter, where, grateful for screw caps, I open the bottle. Pam's wineglasses are on the counter, too, a bright red bow atop them; obviously they are Emma's gift to her. I don't worry about washing them before I pour burgundy liquid into three. I reach over, setting a glass in front of each of my sisters on the small, cottage-blue table. Wine sloshes close to each rim as the table teeters.

Pam looks from me to the glass clutched in my hand and back, her blue eyes full of questions. Unlike Emma, who exercises tact she's had to learn when dealing with exes, hers and his, Pam asks, "What? Looking to drown your sorrows?"

"Hell no, I'm celebrating." I lift the glass and offer a toast to myself instead of drinking to her new life. "I kicked Kitty's ass."

"Massacred is more like it," Emma mutters, just loud enough that I catch it and am reminded of the little girl shopping with her mother.

A twinge of guilt steals some of my triumph. I hope I haven't scarred her for life. But then if this incident keeps her away from the little *killer* cakes, I don't feel bad at all. In fact I feel powerful. Wonder Woman and Charlie's Angels all rolled into one small package.

I can feel my smile against the rim of the glass as I take a sip. The warm, sweet wine joins the laughter bubbling inside me. "Yeah, massacred," I gloat.

"I can't believe you—" Pam chokes out, for maybe the first time in her forty-seven years at a loss for words.

The mayor of our town is a bachelor, so as the bank manager's wife, Pam has been the first lady of Stanville for as many years as Keith's held his position. She's used to maintaining a certain level of decorum, of class, and commanding respect because of that.

That's probably why she and Rob had always clashed. Rob never cared what people thought of him. No, that's not true. He wanted people to think he was fun, and enjoy being around him. He just hadn't cared whether or not they'd respected him.

I wonder how much respect Pam is going to get for leaving her husband and moving into the tiny apartment above The Tearoom. But that's her problem.

Right now she's worried about mine, floundering to find words to no doubt offer her infinite opinions. I'm loving this more and more.

"Yes?" I tease, knowing that somewhere Rob is giving me a thumbs-up.

"You really…"

I catch Emma's gaze, and she starts giggling now. "Oh, yeah, she *really*," she adds to the bizarre conversation, one that would cause anyone eavesdropping to think we'd had more than a sip of wine.

"But Holly, how could—"

"She snapped," Emma says, confirming my suspicion that she had watched the whole thing.

"I snapped," I agree wholeheartedly.

Pam finally finds her voice and an opinion. "I think you better go back to that grief counselor."

But this is the first time in six months I feel like I

don't need counseling. Everyone else might have thought I was doing better, but I didn't. I felt as if I was in a haze, barely able to function.

Until now. I snapped, all right—everything back into place.

The setting sun is painting the lawn gold when I pull into the driveway. I press the button for the garage door, and as it's opening I ease the Tahoe close to the stall on my side of the garage, except now both sides are mine.

Since I loaned Rob's ridiculous orange Beetle to Emma's college-commuting daughter, the garage is empty when I'm not home. Except for tonight. Tonight boxes randomly dot the cement floor. I press on the brakes to keep the Tahoe from crushing them. What's happening now?

Has Keith snapped like I did tonight? Instead of letting Pam take her sweet time moving her things out, has he flung them into boxes and parked them in my garage while he's changing the locks on the house?

She's my sister, and I love her. But I feel nearly as much satisfaction in that as I had in crushing the Kitty Cupcake display.

Rob had often said that Keith needed to grow a set of balls. He always let Pam boss him around, telling him what to wear and how to act. I guess she's like that because she's the oldest, but Emma and I had never put up with her bossiness. Keith, on the other hand, had had no problem with it for twenty-five years.

Pam was the one to leave, although she and Keith had kept that to themselves for a while. Only a few more know it now. She stayed with me after Rob died, helping me through those first few weeks of paralyzing grief. I thought then that I had been her only reason for staying; I hadn't known how unhappy she was in her marriage…until she admitted to needing to get away from it…and Keith.

She might have stayed with us indefinitely if not for Robbie taking over in the prank department for his father. Pam hadn't appreciated his putting cellophane over the toilet seat in the guest bathroom, nor his switching of the hot and cold knobs in the shower. I probably should have gotten upset about his behavior, too, but it had felt good to laugh again. And because of Pam's control-freak tendencies, I hadn't wanted her to stay indefinitely.

So she'd gone back home, but she never returned to Keith's bed, choosing to sleep in her daughter's old room until she could find another place to live. He offered to move out, but Pam wouldn't let him. Since the separation is her idea, she feels she needs to be the one to leave.

I think there's more to her decision than fairness,

though, because she had certainly never worried about that when we were growing up. I think she wants to leave the old farm, like Mom did when Dad died. Pam wants to get away from here and start over completely.

I can't say the thought never crossed my mind during the past six months. But I'm not like Pam. I can't consider just what *I* want. I have to think about the kids, even if they might not always believe that I do.

I park the Tahoe, and as I jump out, I glance across the gravel drive to where Pam's modern house juts behind a stand of pines. The big tinted windows are aglow with the sunset; I can't tell if Keith's home or not. No locksmith truck is parked in the driveway. Maybe they've already been and gone. It's pushing eight o'clock now.

I step over boxes on my way to the side door, which stands open. Light from the kitchen spills into the garage. "Hello?" I call out, a bit nervously. Since Rob's death, I'm not quite sure of the reception I'll get in my own home.

Some garbage bags sit outside the laundry room. I can't believe the kids would have been cleaning while I was gone. They don't do their chores when I'm here, nagging them. Like Pam, they're using Rob's death to excuse some of their behavior.

But maybe that has changed.

"What's going on?" I call out again, when no one joins me in the kitchen. My voice bounces off the antique-white cabinets and oak floor.

From the dirty dishes sitting on the Corian island instead of in the sink, I'm thinking not that much has changed. It's good that the kids ate dinner while I was with my sisters, but they could have cleaned up the mess.

The garbage bags probably contain Pam's clothes, things Keith hadn't felt comfortable leaving in the garage. Even fed up, he could be considerate.

I hear a door open from one of the bedrooms off the hall at the other end of the great room. The master suite is next to the formal dining room, which is separated from the great room, kitchen and breakfast nook area by plaster columns. Rob and I spent a lot of time designing our home so everyone would have their privacy, most especially us.

Claire comes around the corner, her mouth pulled into its perpetual pout. Even with the sulky face, she's a pretty girl with her father's big, dark eyes and my golden-brown hair. I gesture to the dishes on the counter—I think kitchen cleanup was her chore tonight—but she crosses her arms across her blossoming chest instead.

If she's hoping for a reaction, I don't have one for her. Despite having only a half glass of Lambrusco, I'm feeling mellow tonight.

"Ohh, mutiny," I tease her.

She glares at me, a look that threatens that I've seen

nothing yet. Like everyone else, I could blame Rob for her recent change in behavior, but I think hormones might have as much or more to do with it. My mom warned me that this is the age at which my sisters started clashing with her. *I*, of course, was the perfect child.

"She's home!" Claire screeches, and there's pounding as Robbie runs up the steps from the walk-out basement, which is divided into our family room, Rob's den and the guest suite where my son terrorized Pam. I don't have to guess where he was; Robbie's always on the computer in the den and too preoccupied to come when you call him. So why is tonight different?

Uneasiness tightens the knot in my chest, the one that has made it a little hard to breathe since Rob died. I ask again, "What's going on?"

Robbie pushes his glasses up his nose, his big, dark eyes magnified by the thick lenses. At fifteen, he's about the same height as Claire and probably weighs less, even though she's a stick. Unlike his giant of a father, Robbie looks the part of the computer geek, complete with asthma inhaler. Even though he has physical limitations, he's never felt inferior, thanks to all the time and attention Rob gave him. They'd shared so many interests, probably too many considering the pranks Robbie played on his aunt.

And Claire, she'd been the proverbial Daddy's little

girl, his spoiled princess. He'd forever been buying her stuffed animals and candy. I guess I'd been his princess, too, because he'd done the same for me. Of course, he'd eaten more of the candy than I had.

Despite Robbie's and Claire's mulish expressions, my heart softens for my fatherless children, and I start putting the dishes into the sink myself, triumphant all over again for what I did to Smiley's display. Those damn cupcakes deserve far worse for what they stole from us. I wonder where the factory is…?

"Mom!" Rob shouts, drawing my full attention with his urgency. He usually speaks very softly, only raising his voice if Claire's irritating him.

"What?"

"Did you really do it?" he asks, his words quivering with emotion.

Oh, crap. They heard already. Those probably aren't Pam's things packed in boxes and garbage bags; the kids probably packed mine, ready to commit me to the loony bin. How can I explain that the attack was a good thing?

"Who told you?" I ask.

Even though I'm stalling for time, I am also curious about who'd been in the crowd that had gathered for my performance.

Claire and Robbie share a quick glance.

"*You* told us…this morning…when you dropped us

at school." She says each part separately, as if reading a list of my offenses to a judge. Rob and I always said she'll be a lawyer someday.

Since I hadn't planned my victory over cupcake evil in Smiley's, I realize with a quick flash of relief that they're talking about something else. Should I tell them about Smiley's before someone else does?

I answer myself with a shrug. They lived with their father for fifteen and eleven years respectively; they're used to outlandish behavior. Their friends had envied them their "fun" dad. I'm not so sure a crazy mom is envy-inspiring, though.

"So what are we talking about here?" I ask.

"The business." Robbie's speaking through gritted teeth, his braces scraping together due to his overbite.

I wince over what the orthodontist will say at our next appointment.

"Did you really sell it?"

Okay, they still aren't happy with my decision. "I told you why—"

"Told!" Robbie interrupts, his face flushing with bright red blotches. Maybe his acne is flaring up again. "You *tell* us what you're doing. You don't *ask* what we want!"

That's kind of how it works since I'm the parent and they're the children, but I don't say this. I'll let them vent. Tonight.

"It's not fair," Claire chimes in like a backup singer. This is a chorus she's sung often.

"You got rid of Dad's car—"

"Just a loan," I remind them.

When, or should I say *if*, Robbie gets his license, the car will be back in the garage, waiting for him. A five-year-old Volkswagen is a little easier to hang on to than a business.

"And his clothes!"

No matter how much he grows, Robbie would never fit into those. Not that Rob had been obese. He'd been a bear of a man, six feet five with broad shoulders, big all over. I thought we'd all agreed that giving his clothes to the Salvation Army was a good thing, something Rob would have liked, giving help to the recent hurricane victims. Rob was the kind of guy who'd willingly give someone the shirt off his back. In the case of the loud Hawaiian shirts he'd favored, though, no one would probably want those.

"You're getting rid of everything," Claire says, her words followed by a little hiccupping sob.

Robbie straightens up, just a hair taller than his little sister. I don't think I've ever seen him stand as tall as he is now. "We figure you're probably selling the house next, so we started packing our stuff."

So that's what all the boxes and bags are for.

"C'mon, I'm not selling the house."

Not that I hadn't considered it. Living in my dream house without the man who had shared that dream had been a nightmare for a while. Guilt flashes through me, and I think they catch it.

Robbie's face reddens more, and Claire's expression gets sulkier. "You want to get rid of every trace of Dad," he says accusingly.

"It's not fair." Claire sings her familiar chorus. "You've taken everything of Dad's away from us!"

It's not the first time I've heard this; they said it all, not as angrily, though, when I first told them of my intention to sell the business. But this is the first time I hear what they haven't said—that they blame me for taking their father away.

Like I blame Kitty Cupcakes.

And before that the officer who'd brought me the news of Rob's death.

Rob died in a car accident, having crashed his winter-beater, four-wheel drive vehicle into a tree. At first it had looked as if road conditions, icy even in March thanks to Michigan's mercurial weather, might have caused the crash.

I'd sworn at the officer for not making the roads safe to drive, although now I'm pretty sure he hadn't been responsible for that. I think I might have slugged him. In fact, I can't remember exactly what I did.

I'm glad the kids hadn't been home that night. I'd

sent them over to Emma's just a little bit before, to return the kitten they'd taken from her barn and sneaked into the house. I'm grateful they didn't see me like that as I was more out of control than at any other time in my life—what happened in Smiley's doesn't even come close.

After the coroner ruled Rob's death had been caused by a heart attack, I didn't apologize to Deputy Westmoreland. I should, but I don't know what to say.

I don't know what to say to my kids now. I know how much of a release it is to have someone or something else to attack when you're hurting inside, but they can't really blame me for their father's death...unless they think I should have stopped him from eating those cupcakes. Maybe they don't realize how much I tried, and I should try to convince them that I did. But I don't think they're ready to listen to me.

Sometimes you have to let them go....

Despite my sister's advice ringing in my ears, I follow my kids as they rush out of the kitchen and down the hall to their rooms. Ever since six months ago, I've been struggling with that letting-go part of parenting.

Rob's parents wanted the kids to spend a couple of weeks with them this summer, but they live in Indiana, and that was too far away from me. Because of the business, I hadn't been able to be away for that long.

But I know my in-laws are hurting, too, so we compromised, and I brought the kids down for a weekend.

The kids are *not* happy I followed them to their rooms now. They've turned and are glaring at me from just inside their doorways. So I don't make things worse; I stop myself from yelling at them for yelling at me. But I can't think of anything to say in lieu of yelling. *They*, however, don't have that problem.

"I hate you!" they both shout before slamming their doors, in such perfect unison that I wonder if they practiced while I was gone. That opinion is the only one they have shared since thinking macaroni and cheese the perfect side dish to every meal, which is probably only marginally healthier than Kitty Cupcakes.

I know they don't mean it, and that eventually they'll get over this. They're good kids, and we've always been close. But as I head toward my empty master suite at the other side of the house, I don't feel so powerful anymore.

Then I remind myself, Wonder Woman didn't have any kids. Neither did any of Charlie's Angels.

STAGE 3

I notice the sign as I pull out of the driveway. I'm not sure if I missed it the night before, or if they put it up when they headed out to the bus this morning. It's a For Sale sign, Worst Offer, for our once happy home.

Despite the sentiment, or shall I say resentment, behind it, I find myself chuckling. Even though their grades, usually straight A's, have been slipping since school started a few weeks ago, I'm reassured that they're still smart. Asses. But smart.

They might not be doing their homework lately, as much from laziness as taking advantage of their teacher's sympathy over their loss, but they worked last night. Between packing up their stuff and making this sign, they were *very* busy. Mother's pride spreads warmth through my chest, dispelling some of the tightness their angry words had left me with last night.

I glance in the rearview mirror, at the box in the back of the Tahoe, and chuckle louder. As the tires bounce over the ruts in our private dirt road, I imagine the hula girl swaying madly inside the box.

Just inside town, I drive by the drop box for Goodwill. I should leave the lamp there, but for some reason, possibly the guilt trip the kids laid on me last night, I keep driving on through Stanville. With its canopied storefronts and brick sidewalks, it could grace any Christmas card, it's that quaint.

I'm almost to work when I remember I don't work there anymore. Brad asked me to stay on, but I refused, as I don't believe they really want me there. He was just being sweet, and I wouldn't feel right about it; the business is theirs now. I've taken them on as a client, though, for my accounting business. I'll do their book-keeping and payroll, just as I've been doing for my mom's tearoom, from the office I'll have in my house, in Rob's old den. But for the day-to-day stuff, for the past six months I've been training Steve's mom to answer the phones and set appointments.

It's likely the training took so long because of that haze I was in, or maybe she doesn't pick up on things as quickly as her son. Any of the guys could have learned to do those duties themselves, but they may have wanted to keep that maternal influence in the office. For years, I'd been the maternal element.

I miss it now—I'd be lying if I said I didn't—but I won't miss being there without Rob and feeling guilty because he's not. I only worked there to spend time with him. He's the one who loved the place. He started it so he could quit his IT job in the city, save the commute and avoid the travel he'd had to do, and spend more time with his family.

Being at the office since Rob's death only served to remind me that he hadn't been able to live that part of his dream, hadn't been able to spend more time with us. So I actually feel relief that I sold it. I smile as I let the feeling wash over me like the light rain that's falling, washing the dust off the Tahoe.

The kids might be mad now, but in time they'll see it was the right decision, not just for me but for them, too. I'll have more time to spend with them now, since I'll be working from home. I'm not sure how they'll feel about my converting Rob's den, though. But if they're going to heal, they have to accept that he's gone, and they can't do that if I leave everything the same, as if he'll walk through the door any minute and break our tense silence with his big, booming laugh.

I pull into one of the diagonal spaces in front of The Tearoom. I'd been much older than my children, in my early thirties, when my dad died, but I'd resented some of the decisions my mom had made. Selling the farm. Buying this place.

I hadn't understood the stages of grief then. I hadn't *accepted* that Dad wasn't coming back. I'd thought we should keep the farm for *him* because he'd loved it so much.

At that time, I hadn't realized that my mom had to do what was right for *her*, so that she could move on. So that she could find her way past her grief and be there for us again. Hopefully, my kids will understand that someday, as well. Since they're younger than I was when Dad died, I have to be patient, have to give them more time.

When I step through The Tearoom's door, I catch a mad flurry of movement behind the counter. My mother is quickly draping napkins over the pastries in the display case.

Despite the crowd, driven in, no doubt, by the hunger for gossip as much as the rain, the room is dead silent, like Rob's funeral had been when the DJ had played the first few notes of the Stones' "You Can't Always Get What You Want." Rob had loved *The Big Chill* so much he'd worn out two VHS tapes and a DVD of it.

My mother says to me, her small arms spread wide and protectively across the counter, "Please, don't hurt them! They can't defend themselves!"

The room erupts into raucous laughter, just as it had at Rob's funeral. He was only her son by marriage, but they shared a lot of the same traits, such as knowing how to work a room.

I take an exaggerated bow, and everyone applauds.

I'm still laughing as I join her behind the counter, where she grabs me in a fierce hug. I see the concern darkening her blue eyes to navy, and know that what she did wasn't a joke but damage control. For me.

"I'm okay," I tell her.

She arches a golden brow in disbelief. She's dainty and petite, and my dad, although not as big as Rob, had been really strong from all his hard work on the farm. But she was the one we feared as we were growing up. While Dad was easygoing, Mom never let us get away with anything. Then or now.

"I needed to do that," I tell her. "I'm really okay. You *know*."

Nobody knows like she does.

Less than a decade ago, she stood in my shoes. I've found comfort in that, in having her as my little hundred-pound guidebook to widowhood. I tried doing everything she did, moving on like she has, but I couldn't do it *just* like she did. I needed to find my own way…in Smiley's store.

"I know you're okay *now*, sweetie," she says with a smile, and wraps her hand tight around mine.

Not for the first time, I see how similar they are— blue veins running under thin white skin. Initially I noticed at Rob's funeral, when she'd taken my hand in support. They're good hands. Strong, capable hands.

"Thanks, Mom," I say, squeezing hers before releasing it so she can rush off to serve customers.

She needed this place when my dad died. She'd

needed to be needed, to wait on people, to take care of them. With us grown and Dad gone, she'd had no one else to satisfy her desire to nurture.

Coffeepot in one hand, hot water in the other, she pauses on the other side of the counter and turns toward me again. "I have a carrot cake in the back that's been giving me trouble. You want to take care of it?"

Would I ever! With a fork and knife instead of my fists and feet. I'm not a complete militant when it comes to sweets. I have my weaknesses, and my mother knows them. She winks before trotting off.

She's sixty-seven now, but men's heads still turn when she walks past. I don't think it has as much to do with her youthful face and figure or her golden-blond hair and bright eyes as her spirit.

She's indomitable.

I will be, too. I just need to figure out the rest of it. What happened in Smiley's yesterday wasn't planned. As I admitted to my sisters, I just snapped.

I'm sitting at the counter, a pot of fruit-and-almond decaf tea steeping in front of me. Mom always collected tea sets, but the collection had gotten out of control as my dad, my sisters and I had given one to her for every birthday, Mother's Day, Christmas and anniversary. She'd had very little to buy, other than the building, to start her business. I guess she was right, six years ago, when she tried to convince us that selling the farm and starting this tea shop was meant to be.

The pot that sits before me now is one Rob bought for her, a ceramic one with a face like Groucho Marx with the bushy eyebrows, big nose and cigar. I smile at it as I fork small bites of carrot cake into my mouth. I'm savoring the sweet combination of cream cheese and my mother's secret spices when Pam plops down next to me.

"Hypocrite," she mutters as she clutches a mug of coffee between her hands, inhaling the scent of the beans Mom uses.

There's no use talking to Pam until she's had an IV of caffeine in the morning. I might have forgotten that from when we were younger if not for those weeks she stayed with me. Then I'd been careful not to talk to her in the morning, especially if Robbie had played one of his father's pranks on her.

But today I risk it.

"I'm getting a serving of vegetables by eating this. It has carrots in it," I point out.

She shakes her head, then takes a long drink of coffee. With the amount of steam rising from the mug, it's a wonder she doesn't burn her mouth.

I'm in no mood for her silent treatment and try again. "So you *tattled* on me?" I accuse her with heavy mockery.

"Hypocrite," she says again.

"You have a rather limited vocabulary for a woman *your* age," I remark, knowing how much those nine years she has on me bother her. I've been teasing Pam longer than Rob did, even though he was more inventive, but she's always been more amused than annoyed by me.

She's smiling against the mug as she takes a sip; I can tell by the widening of the lipstick marks she leaves on the rim. Pam goes *nowhere* without her makeup. I expect today she needs the armor more than any other.

I want to ask how she enjoyed her first night sleeping alone. But that question brings up painful memories. I didn't sleep in our bed for weeks after Rob died. It was just too big and lonely without him.

"Hey, *you* tattled on *me*," she reminds me.

Although a couple of weeks have passed since I told Mom about Pam's plans, I feel enough guilt to squirm against the leather stool.

Mom's restaurant looks more Irish pub than English tearoom with its rich brown leather stools and chairs, gleaming oak trim and floors and shiny brass fixtures. She did a lot of refurbishing down here, probably working out her anger over Dad's death as I'd worked out mine in Smiley's yesterday. But she'd done nothing with the upstairs, leaving the items the previous owners had stored up there.

"Mom needed to know why we were cleaning out the apartment," I say in my defense.

"And the plan was to tell her that you were going to use it as an office for your bookkeeping since you sold Rob's business," Pam reminds me.

I shake my head. Although I often tease Pam about her age, she hasn't been acting it lately. "*I* was not going to lie to Mom and sneak around behind her back."

"Not perfect little Holly," she agrees, transporting me back to my childhood.

She and Emma had been the ones to lie and sneak around, and because I was younger, they'd excluded me. Or maybe they'd excluded me because I had tattled back then, likely only out of revenge. It hadn't mattered if I'd tattled or not, they always got caught and suffered the consequences.

Like Rob had. I shake off the maudlin thought; I've done enough wallowing. It's time to move on. Maybe Pam has the right idea.

"Did you really think you could move in without her knowing?" I ask.

Pam shrugs, trying for nonchalance even as her face flushes with color. "I just wasn't ready to tell her yet about leaving Keith."

"You worried for nothing. Mom is okay with you staying here. She knows it's just a separation." A very temporary one, I suspect. Pam's been married too long—she doesn't remember how lonely being single is.

She shrugs again.

"Pam? You are going to try to save your marriage, aren't you?"

"I worked on it for twenty-five years, Holly."

Work? Was that what marriage was supposed to be, like a job you labored at twenty-four—seven? Mine hadn't been like that, if you exclude the times I tried to get Rob to eat right. The rest of it had pretty much been a party, full of fun and games and lots of laughter.

Pam expels a weary breath, then adds, "I need a break." From the exasperated look she shoots me, I suspect she doesn't want a break just from her marriage but from her family's questions about it, too. Not that Emma, Mom or I have asked her much about their problems. We hadn't thought they had any, so we've been too shocked by the news to ask.

"Why are *you* here?" she asks me. "Books to do? Don't let me keep you."

I smile at the eagerness in her voice. She obviously wants to get rid of me. "I came to talk to Mom," I say, but don't tell her it's because I need to see if there's a chapter in the widow guidebook about how to deal with resentful children. If I admitted that, Pam might offer advice, or at least an opinion, since she has one about everything. But she really can't understand. She has only one daughter, who was always sweet and loving. Of course Rachael doesn't know her mom left her dad yet. After Rachael married, a little less than a year ago, she moved to the other side of the state, to Detroit, for her husband's job.

"You wanted to warn her about your meltdown in Smiley's," Pam guesses.

"But *someone* already told her about that," I say, glaring at my oldest sister.

"This is Stanville. You expected to keep a secret here?" she asks.

I don't point out that she expected to do the same, and just continue to glare suspiciously at her.

"It wasn't me. I haven't even seen her yet." She turns on her stool and waves at Mom across the room, where she's leaning over a table. All the men over fifty, and some under, are staring at her behind. "Until just now."

I could argue semantics with Pam, that she could have called instead of seeing her, but I know it's not her way of doing things. And if it was, she might not have been the first and certainly wasn't the last to share my Kitty Cupcake coup with Mom.

"I know it wasn't you," I admit, cutting Pam a break.

She's going to need it. When she realizes she made a mistake, I hope Keith gives *her* one and takes her back.

I'm almost relieved now knowing that the boxes and bags in the hall and the garage are full of my stuff, not hers.

The kids said the contents belonged to them, but when I checked, I found towels, blankets and pillows. Their "packing" had consisted of emptying the linen closet.

"It was probably Bulletin Bill," she murmurs around her mug, shrugging a shoulder toward the end of the counter.

Bill Diller is the only man whose head doesn't turn to watch my mother. We figured out when we were kids why that was, that he and our math teacher, Simon Van Otten, who is now the school principal, weren't *just* fishing buddies. But since the locals keep electing Bill mayor, I doubt the rest of our little conservative town knows. They think he's simply a confirmed bachelor. He and Simon are still fishing together exclusively.

As an old-timer gets up to leave, he stops by Bill, patting his shoulder. "Hey, Mayor, I'm going to see if anything's biting since the rain stopped. You gonna let me in on the location of your secret fishing hole?"

Bill laughs and shakes his head, as it's not a secret he's willing to share. But that's the only secret he's ever kept. If I hadn't told Mom about Pam walking out on her marriage, he would have.

"So how was it last night, by yourself?" I ask Pam despite myself.

She's my sister. She was there for me. Even though

I don't agree with what she's doing, I intend to support her.

"Quiet," she says.

I remember those first nights after Rob died. The quiet had been deafening. Now I think back to how many times I jammed my elbow in his side and complained about his snoring until he rolled over, taking most of the blankets with him. What I wouldn't give to lie shivering and wide-awake next to him. I've passed stage five and accepted that's not going to happen. But Pam can still go home.

Before I can suggest it, she releases a deep breath. "It was heaven…."

"What?"

"The silence."

"You liked it?"

"I *loved* it!"

So now is probably not a good time to mention going home to her. I'll wait. She'll get sick of the silence. I know. The kids gave me the silent treatment this morning, and I got sick of it in the amount of time it took them each to shovel down a bowl of cereal and rush out to catch the bus.

Pam jerks so suddenly that coffee sloshes over the rim of her mug. She lets out a soft whistle that only I can hear. When she's with Emma and me, she's not the banker's wife, she's the bossy older sister, but she can also be fun in her way.

My head swivels in the direction of her gaze. I hope it's Keith, looking particularly handsome in one of his dark suits, that has her so interested. But this is a different man, one in uniform. He's not a mailman or a meter reader but the officer the county sheriff assigned to serve and protect Stanville.

"He makes it tempting to break the law," she murmurs.

Deputy Nathan Westmoreland is the man to whom I still owe an apology, and I'm not about to deliver it in front of the crowd in The Tearoom. Despite Mom's damage control, I've already given them enough to talk about.

And talk they will.

If Smiley didn't report me to the police, Bulletin Bill will. On spotting the deputy, who's hard to miss with his wide shoulders and black hair, Bill jumps up from his stool and rushes over to him. The silver glitters around the huge stone of his turquoise ring as he pumps Westmoreland's hand.

Pam and I look at each other and roll our eyes. She shrugs. "I can't fault his taste."

"I hope the principal doesn't catch him," I whisper. "I can't stay," I add, getting up from the stool. I need to do a little damage control of my own and have a few ideas on how to start. I'll pick Mom's brain another time.

As I slip out the door, I turn back and my gaze briefly meets the deputy's. We nod at each other, and I feel my face flush. I really don't care if everyone tells him what happened at Smiley's. He's seen me far more out of control than that.

Claire slams the door so hard that the Tahoe shakes. Then she settles into the back seat without as much as a hello. But at least she's here. Her brother wasn't when I stopped by the high school to pick him up first.

"Hi," I say.

I get nothing but a huffy breath in reply. I'm not sure if that's about last night and she's holding a grudge or if it's just her usual attitude. Since she hit puberty, she lets out more hot air than a ballooning contest.

I understand hormones. I can remember letting out a few of those huffy breaths myself, and I'd been a relatively perfect child, at least compared to my older sisters. But I'm in no mood for her attitude after waiting for Robbie.

"So *you* heard me this morning when I said I'd pick you up from school."

This time she answers me although her tone is not to my liking. "I'm here, aren't I?"

"Oh, yeah, but your brother wasn't."

"*I* have piano."

That's why I always pick her up on Thursdays. Robbie and I usually hang out at the office or The Tearoom until Claire's done with her lesson with the mayor's mother. Mrs. Diller used to be the music teacher at the elementary school when my sisters and I went there.

"Didn't Rob know I was picking him up, too?"

"I guess he didn't feel like waiting."

It's odd that she's defending him. Usually she's tattling on him the way I used to tattle on Pam and Emma.

"So he took the bus home."

No big deal, unless he gets into the special gordita dinner before Claire and I get home. I chopped up all the peppers, tomatoes and onions before I left. Even though I washed my hands, I can smell the onions yet. The leather steering wheel will probably smell like them for some time to come.

I'm not so worried about Robbie eating the healthy things. But if he eats all the strawberry shortcake, his favorite food, before we get home, he'll be in trouble.

"Maybe that's what he did," Claire says, in that I-know-a-secret tone every sister learns. Usually she uses it on *him,* though, not me.

I should be happy that they're getting along, for that hasn't been the case since Claire learned to talk. Like sisters everywhere, she knows which buttons to push for the biggest reaction, and pesters and teases Robbie incessantly. Robbie is typically quiet and mild-mannered; she's always been the only one who can set off his temper…until now.

Now everything's changed. The only reason they seem to be getting along is that they have something in common—being mad at me. I know they're not automatically going to forgive me just because I made their favorite dinner, but it's a start.

Besides, I owe them some homemade dinners. I've been so busy lately with trying to get everything ready for the closing with the business, training Steve's mom, going over records while we waited for all the paperwork to be processed regarding Rob's estate.

It got so bad that Claire and Robbie started complaining about eating pizza *too* much. Maybe Pam's right—I am a hypocrite. Just because my children are both probably underweight doesn't mean that now is not the time to instill healthy eating habits in them. I used to, back when I'd had Rob on that diet.

I remember the days they used to beg for Rob to pick up a pizza on his way home from work. He'd had one with him that night....

"Mom!"

I step on the brakes. "What?"

"You almost passed Mrs. Diller's."

I glance around and see that I am just past the short picket fence that marks her property line. Behind it stands a little white bungalow, its yard aglow with the riotous colors of all the mums she's planted.

Despite her age, Mrs. Diller rises agilely from her

knees and peels off her gardening gloves and floppy straw hat. As Claire hops out to join her without so much as a goodbye, Mrs. Diller waves her hat at me.

I hesitate before pulling away. Robbie's not with me and I'm not sure what to do, so I watch Claire for a moment. I watch the sulkiness leave her face as a smile spreads across it. I watch her snuggle into Mrs. Diller's quick embrace before walking with her into the house. The storm door bounces twice against the frame before closing behind them and shutting me out.

My chest hurts. I want to see that smile on Claire's face again. For me.

"Everyone grieves in his or her own way," the grief counselor had informed me. That was about all she could offer regarding the kids' feelings, since they wouldn't share any of them with her.

Until last night they hadn't shared that much with me, either. The tears in the early days. The shock. The denial. Last night was the first that I've felt their anger. Ironically, the same day I really gave in to mine. Maybe everyone in my house grieves in the same way.

"Give them time," my mother said the day of the funeral and several times since. With the business sold, I can give them *all* my time now. Tonight's dinner is just the beginning.

Since I've waited at the curb so long, I don't have time to drive home and back. I'll let Robbie wait at home—if that's where he is—for a while longer so he can cool off.

Instead I run into town to check on Pam. The outside door for the stairwell to her apartment is locked. She's probably at her yoga class in Grand Rapids, which is about a forty-five-minute drive away from Stanville.

Thinking I might collect some paperwork, I use my key to let myself into The Tearoom. It closes at three-thirty every day. It's only four now, so the air is still rich with the mingled aromas of coffee, herbal teas and cinnamon. I breathe deeply, appreciating now why this place means so much to my mother.

Even empty, it's still abuzz with the chatter from the day, the gossip, which was probably mostly about me. Really, Pam owes me. If not for my incident at Smiley's, folks would have all been talking about her separation.

I wonder how long it took Bulletin Bill to spill the news about me to the deputy. Not long, I'm sure. But I bet Westmoreland wasn't surprised. What does surprise him? He was solemn but not upset the night he brought me the news about Rob.

Westmoreland's not from here, but he's lived in Stanville long enough to be accepted. A few years? I can't remember when he came or where he's from, probably a big city where he's seen far more than a heart-attack-induced traffic accident.

For him that was routine.

For me, it was the end of every routine I've ever known.

I glance at my watch, then lock the door as I leave to pick up Claire. She grunts when I ask her how her lesson went. That's still better than the silent treatment from the morning. Not much, but better.

The house is quiet when we step inside. Some of the bags by the back door are missing. That's good. Robbie's already begun to put some of it away, tantrum over as quickly as mine had passed in Smiley's. Robbie's still my mild-mannered boy.

"Call your brother for dinner," I tell Claire, as I open the fridge and bring out the seasoned strips of steak and chicken, which I've already sautéed. They just need to be popped into the microwave for a quick reheat. I reach for a plate on the counter when my sleeve brushes against something that rustles. A folded piece of paper with "Mom" scrawled across it.

I pick up the note and unfold it.

"Since you're getting rid of everything that reminds you of Dad, I figure you're going to get rid of me next. So I'm saving you the trouble."

STAGE 4

I am not stupid, nor did I raise stupid children. I don't really believe that Robbie has run away.

Despite living in a small town, he is aware of the dangers that might befall a teenager traveling on his own, and because of our small town, traveling would not be easy. The closest bus terminal is a forty-five-minute drive away, the same for the train station and airport.

How would he get to Grand Rapids? Once again, I am glad that I loaned out Rob's Beetle. And because of the asthma that has excused him from every Phys Ed class, I know that Robbie did not *run* away.

If he were truly like his father, this would be one of those pranks he's been pulling lately, and I would open his bedroom door and he'd be standing there with a big grin on his face, thinking he is so funny even though he's not.

But his room is empty.

I know this without even stepping inside because the door is open. His bedroom door is never open.

Neither is Claire's. Hers is shut now, with signs posted all over that No Trespassers Are Allowed. Those *used* to be meant for Robbie. Now I'm not so sure to whom she is referring, but I don't care what she thinks. *I* am not a trespasser in my own home.

I open her door without knocking. She whirls away from her bed, where she is pulling stuff from her backpack. I step close enough that I can see a couple of wadded-up T-shirts and some CDs. Packing or unpacking? Is she intending to leave me a note, too?

"I told you to call Robbie for dinner," I remind her, watching her face.

Her mouth twists into the familiar sulky pout. "I didn't hear you," she claims. The pout becomes a sneer. "I didn't hear you *knock*, either."

I swallow the words threatening to erupt. *This is my house. I don't knock on doors in my own house.* Those were my mother's words whenever Pam or Emma protested her "invading" their privacy. She'd never had to invade mine. I'd never kept any secrets from her. And Claire never used to keep any secrets from me.

She and I had been close...until a few months ago. So much has changed since then. She is no longer my little girl. She's as tall as I am and poised on the brink of adolescence. Even her room reflects this. Not much of the soft yellow walls can be seen through the odd mixture of rock posters and pictures of kitties curled in baskets or hanging from tree limbs. Although she wants to, she's not quite sure *how* to grow up. So she's pushing me, testing her limits.

And mine.

Back when she used to share stuff with me, she'd told me about a friend of hers who purposely makes her mother mad because she thinks it's funny to watch her turn red, and hear her swear. I suspect that is what she and Robbie have been trying with me, not because they think it's funny, but because they're stuck in stage two: anger. They're lashing out like I did in Smiley's.

I am the cupcake now.

"So where is Robbie?" I ask her, ignoring the odd little flutter in my chest. I refuse to panic. There's no reason for it. Robbie has not run away, he's just trying to make a point.

Claire shrugs and looks down at the T-shirts on the unmade bed. "I don't know. Probably downstairs."

In his father's den. He still spends all his time there, playing on the computer. He's not going to be pleased when I take over the room for my office, but Robbie has a laptop he can use anywhere. I need the space for files.

"I don't think he's there," I say, knowing I will check anyway.

"Whatever…"

That is another chorus she sings, like the "it's not fair" one.

"What's with the stuff in your backpack?" I ask her, wanting to know if she thinks she's leaving, too. Is this something they planned together, like the packed bags and boxes and the For Sale sign on the front lawn?

"I got it back from Heather."

She and her friends share clothes and CDs so this is not unusual. But I detect that surly note in her voice, not directed at me for once. "Are you and Heather fighting?"

It would not surprise or disappoint me if Claire said yes. This is the girl who purposely makes her mother mad.

She nods. "Yeah, she's a lying bitch!"

"Claire!" Despite our house rule against swearing, she's called her brother names many times, but never a friend, even a friend like Heather.

"I don't need her." Her dark eyes tell me more, that she doesn't think she needs anyone.

I've wondered why the phone, which used to ring incessantly, has been so quiet. I want to talk to her about this, about her isolation from her friends, because I understand. My friends have stopped calling, too. They expressed their sympathy at the funeral, but now they don't know what to say to me. And if adults can't figure it out, I doubt young girls can.

I want to explain this to her, but don't believe she'll listen to me now. I need to find Robbie and treat them both to their favorite dinner first. I hand her the note.

"What's this?" she asks.

"You tell me." They are too close now for her *not* to know.

She reads it through narrowed eyes. "He ran away?"

"You tell me," I say again. "Earlier, when I asked you about his not riding the bus, you acted like you knew something. Did you know about this?"

"No!" she cries, tossing the note back at me. Her hands are shaking. She's madder now, at him, than at Heather or me. I don't think it's because he ran away but because he ran away *without* her. "All he told me was that he wasn't waiting for you to pick him up. He didn't say anything else. He's a liar!"

She may think she doesn't need anyone, but she's come to depend on her brother. Regardless of their past relationship as pest-pestee, they are the only ones who truly understand what each other is going through, more so than I do. With Rob's passing, I lost my husband; they lost their father.

"I doubt he's really run away," I assure her, as she's blinking back tears. "We'll find him."

I reach to put my arm around her, but she pulls away from me.

"Whatever…"

I am mad now, not worried. I still believe he is too smart to have run away. I'm mad because he's so smart that he has hidden well. He's not with his friends. I have called their houses, had their mothers search their rooms, as I have searched every room of my house.

And the garage.

And the shed in the back.

And now, as I stand at the kitchen window of Emma's farmhouse, I watch flashlight beams bounce around in the woods like huge fireflies. Others are searching for him now.

But he isn't out there.

Autumn, even this early, and his asthma are a bad combination. If he's out among the rotting leaves, he'll be breathing so hard that they'll hear him, the flashlights unnecessary. But it's important to them that they search. Keith is looking, with Emma's husband, Troy, and her oldest son, Dylan. It's how men react; they have to fix things. That was how Rob got into computer repair in the first place. He was a fixer, too.

But his expression would not be as grim as theirs had been when they learned Robbie was missing. He'd be smiling, cracking jokes or sleeping. I remember how he used to play hide-n-go-seek with the kids when they were little. He'd created his own version: hide-n-go-sleep.

While Robbie and Claire hid away, being absolutely quiet so he wouldn't hear them, Rob would lie down on the couch where he'd been counting, and fall asleep.

His snoring would eventually draw them from their hiding places, and he'd catch them when he awoke, without ever leaving the couch.

Maybe I should have tried that. But I'm too mad to sleep. And not just at Robbie for pulling this stunt, but at Rob for not being here to handle it.

My trembling fingers close over one of the ceramic roosters sitting on the windowsill. Like Mom with the teapots, this is what Emma collects, claiming they are required in a country kitchen. While not as bad as the hula lamp, they are tacky. She has too many. Would she mind if I picked up this one and hurled it against the wall? Or through the window? I need to break something so that *I* don't.

Because if Rob were here, Robbie would be, too. He wouldn't run away from his father. *Just me.* I'd thought what he and Claire had said before slamming their bedroom doors last night had been in the heat of the moment, but what if he meant it? What if he hates me? Then he really would have run away....

"Where do you think he could be?" I ask Emma, who stands anxiously behind me. I see her reflection in the glass, the tight expression on her face, the worry in her eyes. It's my face that's staring back at me, the mirror image. There's a catch in my voice as I tell her, "I checked with everyone."

I called my mom on the off chance Robbie walked

to town, but she hadn't seen him. I convinced her not to come out, that the guys had the search under control. Pam still hadn't been home, not that I could see Robbie crashing with his least-favorite aunt. It's probably just out of loyalty to Rob that he doesn't like Pam, and why he played the pranks on her. He'd heard them argue too many times.

Emma puts her arm around my shoulders. Unlike Claire, who'd pulled away from me, I lean into her, appreciating her warmth and support. If only it were Rob's strong arm around me, his big body to lean against for support....

I blink back the tears burning my eyes.

"I don't know," she says.

I was so sure he'd be here, in the old farmhouse where I'd grown up, probably doubting Emma would notice one more teenager with five of them already. Or believing that if she did, she would let him stay anyway.

He and Claire think Emma is more lenient than I am, but that's just because her house has two sets of rules. Emma has one set for her kids; Troy has another for his. And neither of them disciplines the other's. They agreed on this arrangement to protect their marriage. Sometimes I think it does more harm, but Emma will do whatever necessary to make this relationship work, since she really loves Troy.

I understand Emma. I always do. It's Pam who rarely

makes sense to me. Then Emma says, "You need to try Deputy Westmoreland again."

Now I wonder about her. "I didn't call *him*." But I did call the police department. "They're already sending an officer to check the bus and train terminals for a boy matching the description I gave them."

Emma squeezes my shoulder. "Deputy Westmoreland is the one who works with teenagers at the high school."

At-risk teens. Robbie is not at risk. He's just pissed off that I sold his father's business. I'm deliberately obtuse. "Robbie's not at the high school."

I already called Principal Van Otten...at the mayor's house. Robbie had attended school today, but I learned there were some other days that he'd missed.

When I find him, I intend to make it clear to him that skipping school is unacceptable and he has detention to serve. At least I assume that is what Mr. Van Otten wants to discuss during the meeting he scheduled with me for tomorrow, provided I find Robbie by then. I *have* to find Robbie by then. My fingers tighten so hard around the rooster that I imagine I hear a quiet crack. I force my grip to loosen.

Mr. Van Otten also checked with the bus driver and called me back to confirm that Robbie had taken the bus home this afternoon. I doubt he could have gotten as far as the bus or train terminals. He has to be around here somewhere. I continue to watch the lights bouncing around in the woods.

"Holly," Emma says in that long-suffering, patient tone that has me squirming like one of her children. "Deputy Westmoreland knows where all the teenagers hang out."

"I'm sure he's not the only one in the police department who knows. *I* know."

The cemetery. The park. The football field. Nothing much changes in Stanville, or Standstill, which is what we called it as kids, which is what the kids call it now. "I'll go look for him."

"You should stay here," she insists. "In case he comes home."

He better. And soon. Once he does, he'll never run away again because he won't be leaving the house. Maybe I'll homeschool, then I won't have to worry about his skipping or running away. I have the time now.

But Rob will haunt me. He had strong opinions about kids needing the social aspect of public school, especially someone like Robbie, who's so shy. Too shy to be hanging out at the cemetery. Or the park. Or the football field. Looking for him at any of those places would be a waste of time.

"Deputy Westmoreland knows what Robbie looks like," Emma continues. "He was at Rob's funeral."

I'll have to take her word for it, since I didn't see him

there. I really don't care who looks for Robbie, as long as someone is. "I called the police," I remind her again. "And I have pictures of him, you know."

His class photos had come back earlier this week. Maybe I shouldn't have paid extra for the professional touch-up. His skin isn't really that clear, but still they'll be able to recognize him. If it comes to that.

I hope it doesn't. But if they can't find Robbie outside, I need to call the kind-voiced police dispatcher back and have them send an officer out so I can file an official report. A missing person's report.

My son is missing. For a moment I can't breathe, my lungs crushed from the pressure on my chest. I can't lose Robbie, too. I need to do something. I'm tired of standing here, watching other people search for my son. "Do you have another flashlight?" I ask Emma.

She shakes her head. "Come on, Holly. You know he's not out there."

I know he's not. Robbie hates camping, probably because of his asthma. The outdoors, campfire thing was never for him, and our family vacations were all spent in nice hotels.

"He must have new friends," I say, "because he hasn't spent much time with the ones he used to have."

Like Claire, does he think he doesn't need them? But I actually like Robbie's friends. They're sweet and shy like him, like he used to be.

"I'll ask Jason," Emma says. Jason is her stepson who's in the same grade as Robbie, even though he's a year older. Before she leaves the kitchen, she presses a card into my hand. "His cell phone number is on here. Call *him*."

I open my fingers around the ivory paper. Deputy Westmoreland's name and badge number are on the card, along with the number for the police department that I've already called. Someone has also written in his cell number. From the bold scrawl, I figure he wrote it down himself.

When did Emma get this? At the funeral? Had the deputy thought then that Robbie would be "at risk" just because his father had died? Now I'm mad at Westmoreland again. Or still. I can't remember which, but he really has *no* business getting in *my* business.

If I call him, I would tell him that and…that my son is missing. Emma's right. He should be the officer with whom I file the "official" report. He knows the situation, unlike the dispatcher, who'd been kind but not particularly concerned. "He's a teenage boy," he'd said. "He's probably hanging out with friends. But we can take a report…."

I'd held off then, wanting to let the guys finish their search first, but I can't wait any longer. Turning away from the window, I cross to where Emma's cordless phone sits on the counter. It's still warm from all the calls I made earlier. I've punched in two numbers when a clamor erupts upstairs. Raised voices. Jason's. Then Emma's. Emma hardly ever raises her voice. Then there are footsteps on the stairs.

"You aren't supposed to come into my room!" Jason's shouting.

Unlike me, Emma is sometimes considered a trespasser in her own house because of the house rules. She's not allowed to enter Troy's kids' rooms. He respects their privacy, sometimes more than I think he respects Emma. Rob and I hadn't parented like that. We'd been equal partners, which is probably why it's so hard going it alone.

"What's going on?" I ask, as she charges back into the kitchen.

Her face is red, and she's dragging someone—Jason?—behind her. All I see is an arm. Then the rest of the slight body follows.

"Robbie!"

Relief floods me. Until this moment I didn't think I was worried, not really worried, but my knees are a little weak now. If I'd lost him, too…

I reach for him to throw my arms around him, but he steps back. His reaction isn't the same as Claire's rejection of my comfort, though, because there's something in his dark eyes, a fear of me magnified by his thick lenses, that's never been there before.

Maybe it's good that he fears me a little. He should

after this stunt he's pulled. My hands are shaking as I close them over his shoulders, forcing him to look at me.

"What—" I bite my tongue. Damn our no-swearing rule "—were you thinking?"

"I want to live here," he says, "with Aunt Emma."

Pain grips my heart, squashing it as viciously as I had the Kitty Cupcakes yesterday.

Emma flashes me a look, one full of sympathy. As a mother she knows how much it hurts to have your child want to run away from you.

"That's too bad," I say, steeling my voice to cover the hurt. "We all want things we can't have."

I can't have Rob back.

That's what Robbie's and Claire's attitudes are all about. They blame me. Last night I let them. Tonight is another story—my patience has worn out.

That's why I can't homeschool. Rob's wrath and socialization aside, I don't have enough patience, not where my children are concerned.

Seeing that he'll get nowhere with me, Robbie turns back to Emma. "Please, Aunt Em, I can't live with *her* anymore. She doesn't really want me there."

And that's why the fear is there. He's scared that I really don't want him.

"Don't make me go back," he begs.

Poor Emma, always stuck in the middle. I can see her

soft heart in her eyes as she stares back at Robbie. "I'm sorry, honey…."

"She has too many kids already," I remind them both.

At least one too many. Jason has come downstairs now, standing in the doorway behind Emma and Robbie. His hair is dyed black and his eyebrow, nose and lip are pierced. He's only sixteen, but his father gave his permission for the self-mutilation.

With a little relief, I realize that the deputy probably did not give his card to Emma for me or Robbie. Robbie is not the at-risk teen.

Not yet.

But I have a horrible feeling that if I can't reach him, he soon will be.

"Great," Claire says, as she flops onto the living room couch next to Robbie. "It's your fault we gotta listen to a lecture now."

She shifts against the deep suede cushions and manages to elbow him in the ribs, a move both daring, because she does it in front of me, and subtle, because she can swear it was an accident. She's good.

But then so am I. I paid attention growing up. I know what nonsense my sisters pulled on my parents. And I'm not going to let my children pull it on me. Rob and I had made that pact, along with others. Like we wouldn't let them play us off against each other. No going to Dad with a request that Mom had already refused. We had vowed to keep a united front. That's hard to do alone.

"Okay," I say. "We need to talk."

"You mean *you* need to talk," Robbie says. "All *we* get to do is listen."

"That would be nice," I reply, "but apparently you don't do that very well."

His face flushes bright red.

Claire elbows him again. "Dork."

"Enough," I say. And I mean it.

"That's another reason I want to live with Aunt Emma," Robbie says. "Because *she* doesn't." He scowls at Claire.

Their truce of the night before is apparently short-lived. I don't mind. I know they need each other, but I'm not crazy about their ganging up on me.

Rob got a vasectomy after we had Claire because, as he pointed out, we didn't want them outnumbering us. *Well, Rob, they outnumber me now. If only you'd put down the damn cupcakes.*

"You're not going to live with Aunt Emma, either," I remind him. "You live here. And Claire lives here and so do I. This is our home."

That was why I never seriously considered getting rid of it. Even though it's sometimes difficult for me to be here without Rob, I know it would be harder for the kids *not* to be here.

"I'm not selling the house. I'm not getting rid of anything else."

Except the lamp.

I will get rid of the lamp. I wound up bringing it into the house and stowing it in my closet, but just for now because I was going grocery shopping and needed the room in the back. The thing is tacky and impractical and dangerous. It has to go. But that will be the last thing.

"There's nothing else to get rid of," Claire says, unaware of the lamp.

"Just us." Robbie reminds her, and me, of his note.

"I would never get rid of either of you." My voice cracks as I say this, and I blink hard, fighting tears that have sprung up from nowhere, or maybe from the tightness in my chest. "I love you both very much."

They look down, maybe embarrassed to say it back to me with the other listening. I hope that's the only reason they don't reciprocate. We used to profess our love to one another every night at bedtime when they were younger. Losing their father has aged them.

I hope that's all it is. I hope that they don't hate me, as they professed last night to the accompaniment of slamming doors. Do they resent me for being alive instead of their father? Would they have preferred him as the single parent?

Pain presses hard on my heart, stealing my breath for a moment. I'm not jealous of their love for Rob; I still love him, too. I can't deny that he would probably be handling this better than I am. He would find a way to keep them close, instead of pushing them away.

I open up myself more. They deserve that. I spent too long in a haze, unaware of the anger building in them.

"I also *need* you both. That's why you're not running away...or moving out."

"Running away was stupid," Claire tells her brother.

This time he blocks her elbow before she can make her move. But if he had included her in his plan, I doubt she would be as critical of it.

"That was stupid," I agree. "But you're not the only one who's done something idiotic...."

"You're admitting that selling the business was a dumb idea?" Robbie asks, his dark eyes filling with hope, probably that I can back out of the sale.

I shake my head, then suck it up and tell them about what I did in Smiley's.

Claire's mouth falls open. "It's true? I thought Heather was lying."

Robbie starts laughing. "I don't believe it...."

It's the first time I've heard him laugh in ages. Even when he'd pulled those pranks on Pam, he hadn't thought they were funny. Despite my face being hot with embarrassment now, I'm glad I confessed. I haven't felt this close to my children in a long time, not since we held hands beside their father's casket as the DJ played the Rolling Stones.

"But why?" Claire asks, not as amused as her brother. She's appalled that her mother would make such a scene. She's becoming more like her aunt Pam every day. "Why'd you do it?"

I can't talk to them about losing control, about snapping. They need security right now. But anger they do understand. "If your father hadn't eaten so many of those things…"

Robbie's laughter dies. And so does our closeness. "He might be alive," he says.

"I tried to get him to stop," I tell them, hoping they'll forgive me for their father dying and for my being alive instead.

They don't say anything or even look at me. They're both staring at the floor. Fighting back tears?

It's been six months. Why is it still so hard? Shouldn't we be moving on? Shouldn't we be getting better, not worse?

"Can we go to bed now?" Claire asks, getting up from the couch.

Not knowing how else to try to reach them, I nod in agreement. "Yes, you have school in the morning."

Robbie stands, too.

"No skipping," I say, to let him know I know.

But his skipping school is the least of my concerns right now. As I watch my children walk to their rooms, I drop onto the couch and sink deep into the cushions. Despite the warmth and softness, it doesn't compare to the comfort of Rob's arms after a long, tiring day. I'd rather be laying my head against his chest than against a pillow.

But he's gone. And tonight, for a little while, so was Robbie. He didn't go far, just next door. This time. What if he runs again? Or Claire does?

That weak, helpless feeling steals over me once more, the one I felt standing in Emma's window, watching the guys search for my son. I wish I had that rooster in my hands again; I'd twist its head off. I need to do *something*. So I clench my hands into fists and pummel the couch cushion. I'm biting my lip so no grunts or groans slip out, but I'm panting from the exertion. I was already exhausted. Emotionally. Now I'm physically exhausted, too.

I don't know why I can't reach them. We all want the same thing—Rob back. The only difference is that I've accepted he can't come back.

I have to help them get through this. Since I don't have Rob's creativity to help me figure out how, I'll have to do it myself. I can't lose them, too.

STAGE 5

Principal Van Otten's office is so elegantly decorated that I doubt anyone finds it much of a hardship to be sent here. The walls are painted a deep burgundy with that special technique that makes the texture look so much like suede or velvet that I reach out to touch one. The mahogany desk, as well as the black leather chair, are certainly his own special purchases.

Even though I'd never been to this office when I was a kid, I'm sure it didn't look like this when I went to school here. I'll have to ask Pam or Emma. They were sent a few times—pre-Van Otten—Pam for talking back, Emma for hanging with a bad boy.

Why am I here for Robbie? The skipping?

"I'm so glad you found your son, Holly," Mr. Van Otten says with an exaggerated sigh of relief.

While he might refer to other parents as Mr. or Mrs., I was one of his students. I will always be Holly to him. There's something comforting about that, as well as a little frustrating. He will never treat me with the respect he gives to those parents he hasn't watched pass awkwardly through adolescence.

Instead of respect, I get pity, as he gives me *that* look, the one with his head tilted slightly and his eyes soft with sympathy. I've seen that look from just about every resident of Stanville except my family—*they* know how much I hate it.

"You've been dealing with so much," he says softly. "Then Robbie runs away…"

I laugh off his pity with a chuckle that sounds strained even to my ears. "Well, he didn't run far, just to my sister Emma's."

"He was acting out his grief."

More like his anger at me, but I don't correct Van Otten. "Probably."

"He's been doing it at school, too, Holly."

"By skipping?" If so, then he's actually not acting it out *at* school, but I do wonder where he's going when he takes off. "I wish you would have called me about that earlier."

I could have made sure the boy got to school and stayed there. Obviously I can't trust him to get on the bus by himself anymore. Now that I have time, I think I'll start driving him and his sister to and from school regularly. The greatest aspect about self-employment is that I can set a flexible schedule.

"You and those kids have been through so much with losing Rob, Holly."

I nod. He's already said this. He's already offered his pity. I don't want it.

"I wanted to give the boy a break."

"By skipping school, I think he's been giving himself a break," I point out.

"He hasn't just been skipping school," Mr. Van Otten adds reluctantly.

He can't meet my gaze, staring instead at the gleaming surface of his highly polished mahogany desk. Not a paper sits atop it. He's much more organized than I ever was at the business.

Rob used to laugh at the toppling piles I'd spread across the surface of my desk. He'd mock me for being such a Martha Stewart at home and a slob at work. I'd told him that I was just trying to fit in with him. He'd had so much stuff in that office that I hadn't even noticed he stashed that hula lamp there instead of getting rid of it.

I pulled her out this morning from where I'd hidden her in the top of my closet. Watching her sway back and forth eased the tightness in my chest that Robbie's running away had brought me.

I feel it returning now as I ask, "So what else has he been doing?"

Mr. Van Otten reaches across his desk to where I clasp the edge of it. He gives my shaking hand a comforting squeeze much like my mother often does.

"Nothing too serious, Holly. Just pranks. Peanut

butter on locker handles. Cellophane used…" his face reddens "…in the girls' bathroom."

I know how. I'm not as mad at Robbie as I am at Rob right now. *You set some example for our children, hon.*

In my mind I see his big shoulders shrugging and the smile lightening his dark eyes even as he tries to keep it off his lips. I want to yell at him that it's *not* funny. But it is…a little bit. I remember Pam's shrieks when he pulled the pranks on her.

"It's not serious, hardly destruction of school property," Van Otten admits.

The tightness in my chest eases a bit.

"But there are some students with peanut allergies—"

"No one was hurt?" I'm anxious to know.

"Some of the girls had to call home for…" he touches the silk tie knotted perfectly at his throat "…a change of clothes. But other than that, no."

"Are you going to expel him?" I ask, worried that I might be homeschooling yet.

He shakes his head. "Truthfully, we have no proof that he's the one who perpetrated these pranks."

I do. Just as my mother is serving as my guide to widowhood, Robbie's dead father is serving as his guide to troublemaking. If the man wasn't already dead…

"So," the principal continues, "the only offense we can punish him for is skipping school."

"And his punishment?" I ask, wondering if it'll punish me, too. That's one of the side effects of parenting—it seems we always serve our children's sentences with them.

"Detention," he says.

And my punishment is another trip into town to retrieve him from the school as he's serving it. "For how long?"

"A week, after school."

I don't protest. It's better than expulsion. I've never understood why it states in the *Stanville High School Student Handbook* that one of the punishments imposed for skipping school is a three-day suspension.

Isn't that more a reward than a punishment, since teachers are giving students exactly what they've wanted in the first place, *not* to go to school?

"I hope that doesn't seem too harsh," the principal says quickly, his words rushing together. "His teachers and I have tried to be understanding, to give the poor kid a break...."

There's that pity again. I grit my teeth and force a smile. "I appreciate that, but it's been six months. It's time for things to get back to normal."

Even as I say it, I know how impossible that is. With Rob gone, things will never be "normal" for our children and me. Heck, they were never "normal" when he was alive, thanks to his bizarre sense of humor.

But I'll figure something out, something so that they're not running away or getting detention.

I have to.

Sweat beads on my brow despite the cool air. I pump my arms hard, as if I'm about to take flight, as I pick up the pace. I keep my head down, not needing to see where I'm going. I know this route well. My sisters and I used to do this mile-long walk to the bus stop every schoolday when I was a kid.

Now we walk farther than a mile, on the same gravel road, three nights a week. When we were younger, there used to be open fields—my dad's fields, used to feed his dairy cows—on either side of it.

Since his death each field has been split into two-and-a-half-acre lots, and huge houses in brick, stucco or clapboard sit in the middle of each. Although the houses are large, mainly retired couples, who finally have the money to afford their dream homes now that their kids are gone, own them.

Rob and I had only been able to buy ours because my mom sold these fields when Dad died. Pam and Keith also built their dream home with that inheritance. Emma got the old farmhouse, and still we resented Mom for selling the farm.

I'd like to think we all got over it, but sometimes, even now, walking past these houses where Dad's fields had been bothers me. Because I know how much it would bother him—he loved the farm so much.

"Are…*you*…trying to run away…?" Emma asks between gasps for breath as she struggles to keep up with me.

I ease off and turn around, walking backward as she catches up. "I'm thinking about it," I admit.

Not much has changed since my visit to the principal's office over a week ago. Robbie has served out his sentence, but I expect it won't be long before another punishment is imposed on him.

The kids are not as openly angry as they were right after I sold the business. Now they're more into quiet resentment. I try to hold them closer, driving them to school, spending every night with them, but I still feel them slipping away from me.

Unfortunately, I can't lash out at the person who's responsible for this distance between us. That person is already dead.

Emma laughs. "You and me both."

"What?"

"I want to run away, too," she says, but I think *she* means it.

"What's going on?" I ask, noticing the lines of strain around Emma's mouth and the dark circles under her eyes.

Before she can answer, someone shouts, and a flurry

of yellow velour rushes toward us. Fallen leaves and dust from the dirt road kick up from the heels of Pam's Keds. I've never seen her move so fast.

"So…now…you're walking *without* me!" Pam accuses as she joins us, her blue eyes dark navy with anger.

Emma and I share a quick glance.

"We didn't know you were going to join us," I answer for both of us, since lately I've had the most experience dealing with angry people.

"We walk the same three nights every week," she says, as if we're too stupid to remember. Condescension is another trait of an oldest sibling. "I left my *husband*, not my *family*."

But the first two nights this week, she didn't join us. She'd been busy in Grand Rapids, shopping, taking her yoga class. I don't point this out to her, though, but I can see from Emma's expression that she's thinking the same thing.

"We know that, honey," Emma says, in the same tone she used to talk to her children when they were toddlers, and tired and temperamental. If I remember correctly, she used that same voice on me those first few weeks after Rob died.

"You don't act like it," Pam sharply retorts, shaking her head and ruffling her bob around her chin.

I don't possess a tenth of Emma's patience.

"Why do you have a bug up your ass?" I ask. I'm more

like Pam in the tact department, sorely lacking, at least with my sisters, especially after the week I've had.

"*You* should know," she says, stepping close to me. She's actually an inch shorter than I am, so she shouldn't be intimidating. But she's still my *big* sister.

"So you're mad at *me?*" Why am I surprised? Everyone else is. I can't shop at Smiley's anymore without him following me from aisle to aisle.

She nods, just a quick jerk of her head.

"What did I do to you?" As far as I know, I haven't gotten rid of anything she valued. Not even Rob. And now I'm mad at her.

"How could you…" she sputters, nearly as flustered as she was at her housewarming party.

"How could I what?"

Emma's standing there, her gaze swinging back and forth between the two of us, her eyes wide with fascination. Usually she hates conflict and plays peacemaker for us. Today she just watches. That letting-go part of parenting again? She tries to mother everyone if they'll let her.

Maybe Pam has more tact than I thought because she begins, "When Robbie went missing—"

"The boy ran away," I'm not too proud to admit. I won't admit that the thought of his doing it again keeps me awake nights. They don't need to know how worried I am, since they'd only worry, too, and they've done enough of that over me the past six months. "So what about it?"

Pam's voice is trembling with accusation as she replies, "You called Keith."

"Yeah?"

"But…"

"I called you, too, Pam, several times. You weren't home, and you don't have a cell phone." Which is the continuation of another argument between us. I think it's irresponsible not to own one, but she always says that she doesn't want to be bothered with phone calls unless she's making them. Even after Rob's flat-tire prank, she wouldn't admit she's wrong about needing one.

She's still sputtering. "But you called *Keith*."

I'm failing to understand why she's so upset. "He's still my brother-in-law."

"Not for long," she says. "I filed."

With those two words, her anger evaporates, as does mine.

Emma sighs. "You filed? But I thought…"

"You were only separating," I finish when she can't. "That you just needed a break."

"I knew you were thinking about it," Emma continues. "You wouldn't have left if you weren't." She's been divorced so she would know.

"I thought about it," Pam says, and she starts walking. We follow, but our pace is slower.

"Is that all you've done?" I ask, my temper flaring. How dare she give up that easily! "What about counseling?"

"We already tried counseling," she says, "years ago."

Her revelation stuns me. I glance at Emma, whose openmouthed stare reveals she's equally as floored. "You never said anything…."

Pam's face flushes, and not from the speed-walking. "It was personal."

It was pride. I know it, but I don't call her on it as I understand what she's feeling. It's why I'm trying so hard to stand on my own two feet.

"So get back into it," I insist.

She shakes her head. "It won't fix what's wrong with us."

"So what's wrong with *you?*" I can't figure out why she won't fight. I wish I'd fought Rob harder to put down the cupcakes. I wish a lot of impossible things.

"You should think about this some more," Emma ventures. "Give it more time—"

"It's been twenty-five years," Pam replies, as if she's speaking of a life sentence. But if it were, she wouldn't be up for parole yet.

"I'm not talking about your marriage. I'm talking about your separation," Emma says, her tone sharp. She's angry now, and we both stop walking to stare at her. It takes a lot to make Emma angry, like a punked-out teenage stepson hiding my runaway in her house. "How can you just throw away twenty-five years?"

"Of everyone, I thought *you* would understand," Pam says to Emma.

"I didn't choose to get a divorce," Emma reminds us, but she was the one who'd filed.

Of course, Gord had already been gone a long time by then. I'm not sure if he really deserted her, or if he just got so drunk, he couldn't remember where they lived. That had happened more than a few times. Eventually he came back, after the divorce, and he sees the kids from time to time—when he's not drinking too much, which isn't often.

Shame washes over me at all my anger toward Rob. He'd had only one bad habit, and he'd come home every night…except that last one.

"But you couldn't stay married," Pam argues. "Like I can't stay married."

"Why?" I ask. "Keith is a great guy."

"Then *you* marry him," Pam says, waving her arms in exasperation. "He'll be single soon." Then she adds with great satisfaction, "And so will I."

I drag in a quick breath so that I don't yell at her. She can be such a bitch sometimes. But she's my sister. And this is what she wants…for whatever crazy reason. Still I have to ask, "Are you *sure* this is what you want?"

"I've thought about this for a long time," she says quietly. "I just didn't have the guts to do it until now."

Could Rob have been wrong all these years? Was it Pam who had needed to grow the set of balls, not Keith? I shake my head in denial. She's one of the toughest women I know. "Pam, that doesn't make any sense."

"He's a great guy. You all say it. *You* all love him. But *I* don't. I haven't for a long time. Counseling can't make you love someone. I stayed for Rachael, so that she could have both parents. Then, even after she got married and left—" she sighed "—I stayed because I didn't know how to leave...."

Her voice catches with tears, and I know now why she's been unhappy all these years. It wasn't that she didn't know how to be happy; she *knew* how. She was just too scared to do what she had to to *be* happy.

I pull her close and hug her. "It's okay, Pam. You do what you have to do. We'll be here for you."

I'm saying all the right words, but I can't help my selfish thoughts as resentment heats my blood. A part of me hates her. How can she just throw away her marriage, her husband, when I'd do anything to have mine back?

I shut my bedroom door carefully so that the oak settles softly against the frame, then I click the lock. I need a break. The kids are squabbling over what program to watch. We have more than one TV. One of them could go down to the family room, but they'd rather fight. In some ways that should make things seem normal again, but there's something different to their fighting now. Before, they'd been teasing or mildly annoyed. Now they're really angry.

I brought them back to the grief counselor to discuss this, but they subjected her to the same silent treatment I mostly get from them. Of course, the silence is preferable to their arguing.

I take a deep breath, enjoying the serenity of my bedroom with its pale green walls and oak trim. My feet sink into the plush beige carpeting as I cross the room to the walk-in closet.

When I step inside, I'm not looking for something to wear. I'm already in my flannel pajamas, warm and comfy. Whenever I wore them around Rob, he had called me "Grandma." Then he'd go on about my eyes…and other body parts. Now that I don't have him to keep me warm, I'm determined not to freeze. Along with his Hawaiian shirts and 36-long pants, I packed off the presents he'd bought me from Victoria's Secret. They'd only been fun to wear for him, when they hadn't actually stayed on long enough to scratch, ride up and chafe.

Like every other aspect of his life, Rob had been fun in bed, too. I wrap my arms tight around my middle, feeling hollow. Empty.

God, I miss him.

I probably should have shared that with the grief counselor, but I hadn't talked any more to her than the kids had. And I hadn't really heard whatever she'd said to me. Probably something about all those stages again. I already know each of them as intimately as I'd once known Rob. Her words had sounded as warbled as that of the teacher from Peanuts. I can hear her voice murmuring now, under the door, as the TV set blares "It's the Great Pumpkin, Charlie Brown."

It had been one of Rob's favorite cartoons. Robbie's claiming it's one of his. Claire's protesting that she's too old to watch a little kids' show.

I can't talk to them; I've tried. I can't talk to the counselor. But honestly, I really didn't try.

There's only one person I *can* talk to.

Using my foot, I drag over the oak stool to stand on so I can reach the shelf above the clothes. It's hell to be short. I wrestle down a cardboard box and carry it over to the bed to take out that horribly tacky, fire-hazard lamp. She sways back and forth, with that serene smile painted on her lips. I run my fingers over her silky black hair, straightening the tresses.

And I feel close to Rob.

It's ridiculous, really.

I'm ridiculous.

Most people visit the cemetery when they want to

feel close to their departed loved one. I take out this lamp. I've been doing it almost every day over the past couple of weeks.

Every time I see her smile, I smile, too. It's like when a stranger smiles when they pass you on the street—you automatically smile back. Well, maybe not everyone does that, but I do. Sometimes that's all I need, that quick smile. Other times, like tonight, I find myself talking to the lamp. But I'm really talking to Rob.

"What do I do about the kids?"

I've tried all the old methods to cheer them up. Favorite foods, trips to the mall, movies, buying the newest video games—nothing has worked. I know what they're going through is worse than a bad grade or no invitation to a party, but I don't know what else to do.

Rob doesn't offer any suggestions. Neither does the lamp; it just sways back and forth. I know I can't give up, because Rob wouldn't have. If he'd been a quitter, we wouldn't have ever gotten together. But then again, if he'd been a quitter and had stopped eating those cupcakes, we might still *be* together.

But I can't blame him anymore. Not for dying and not for this distance between me and the kids. It's as much my fault. If I hadn't been in such a haze the first six months, I might have reached them already. I'd thought I was doing what was best with the counseling, with handling Rob's estate, so that I'd have more time with them, which I do.

I wish I had more time with Rob.

But I realized something when Pam was talking the other day. I would rather have what I did—seventeen years of happiness—than twenty-five years of unhappiness.

"I'm a lucky woman," I say to him, as I'd told him so many times before.

The lamp nods in agreement.

My doorknob rattles. "Mom!" Claire screeches. "Is this locked?"

I scramble to put the lamp back in the box, then slide it onto the closet floor. I swing that door closed with my foot before crossing the room to open the other.

"Robbie hid the remote," Claire says. "He's such a dork. Tell him to give it back. I want to change the channel."

Which is probably why he hid it.

"You know," I say, following her from my bedroom, "there is actually a way to change the channel without the remote."

As she heads to the great room, she looks back over her shoulder at me, her eyes full of disbelief.

I laugh, and for just a second think I hear an echo bouncing off the vaulted ceiling. Rob's laughter. He'd love this.

"No, really," I swear. "You can change the channel on the television."

"I want the remote," she says.

Robbie won't reveal its hiding place, and Claire isn't interested in working the television manually. The argument escalates until I send them both to their rooms. They're not two anymore, and I can't keep giving them time-outs.

And I can't put them in a box and pack them away in the closet, either. I need more from Rob than the echo of his laughter. I need answers. But I know I'm only going to find those within myself.

STAGE 6

"**I** need to get away for a while," Pam says, settling onto the stool next to me at The Tearoom counter.

You and me both. After dropping the kids off at school, I stopped here to pick up some paperwork, write some checks and steal Mom away from her customers for a while to pump her for advice. But as soon as somebody leaves, two more come in. All I've managed is some bookkeeping.

"Busy place," I say to Pam, gathering up the papers I spread across the counter. I need more space to work, but don't think the kids are ready yet for me to take over Rob's den.

Pam's been helping here since she moved into the apartment. I think it's her way to compensate for Mom not charging her rent. But she's not like our mother, out mingling with the customers. She's either in the kitchen baking or behind the counter making coffee.

There is another waitress, Nina, but even with her

and Mom, Pam could be out in the dining area, helping. Instead she seems to hide.

"Too busy," she says with a heavy sigh.

I figure she's changing her mind about living above the business, maybe even changing her mind about filing.

"Is everything all right?" I ask.

If she stayed unhappily married for twenty-five years because she was scared, she'll probably be too scared to admit she's changed her mind.

She nods. "I'm fine."

"You're not. Have you told Mom yet—"

She lifts a finger against her lips. Only Emma, Keith and I know that she's filed, and we've all been sworn to secrecy.

"But I did tell Rachael," she says, and I see the glint of tears in her eyes.

I bet it would have been easier to tell Mom, who will support Pam even though she'll be disappointed. "She didn't take it well?"

"My daughter hates me."

I can identify with that. Even though they haven't said it again, I suspect my children still hate *me*. Hurt and guilt flash through me simultaneously, and I remember that in addition to the talk of stages, the counselor had mentioned something about survivor's guilt. But I can't think about myself now; Pam's hurting.

"She won't talk to me to let me explain." Pam shrugs,

trying to act as if it doesn't bother her. But she and Rachael were always so close, as much friends as mother and daughter. "She's a newlywed. She doesn't understand that you can't stay that much in love. That it doesn't last."

It doesn't? I could argue with her. My love lasted seventeen years and even now, beyond the grave. Love, real love, lasts. But then isn't that the point Pam's trying to make?

I sigh as my resentment drains away. "I'm sorry, Pam." Then, because she'd been there for me, I ask, "Is there anything I can do?"

She blinks away the hint of tears, her eyes brightening. "I'd really like to get away for a while...."

"Okay." Maybe she intends to go see Rachael, to try to have that talk her daughter is denying her. "To Detroit?"

She shakes her head. "Neither of us is ready for that. No, I really want to get *away*."

"That might be a good idea." Give her perspective, so that she can see Keith is a good man and her marriage is worth working on. "So what's stopping you?"

Maybe she doesn't want to go alone.

"You can see how busy this place is," she says. "I wouldn't feel right about not helping Mom."

I don't point out that it doesn't look as if she helps

her much. "Don't worry about it. Mom should probably hire some extra help anyways."

Pam shakes her head. "I don't want someone to permanently take my job. I want to work here. It's just..."

"It's just *what?*" I ask.

"You're lucky to be a widow."

Just when I think nothing Pam does or says will shock me, she comes up with something that has me clenching my hands so I don't slap her. I slam my fists against the counter. The Formica surface isn't as forgiving as the couch cushions. Pain licks up from my knuckles throughout my fingers and into my wrists. But it doesn't hurt as much as my heart. "What the hell—"

Is it the money? Did Keith tell her about all the zeroes? Does she think *any* amount of money can compensate for what I lost?

My kids lost the father they adored. I lost my husband, my lover, my best friend. You can't put a price on what Rob meant to us. But I can't express any of this to Pam. If I open my mouth again, the sobs burning my throat are going to gurgle out. It's not pride stopping me, as it's stopped her so many times. It's the fear that once I start, I may not be able to stop.

"I'm sorry, Holly," she says, her eyes full of sincere regret. "I don't mean it like that. I know you miss Rob." She hides it well, but I bet she wonders why.

I wait for whatever she's struggling to say, still not trusting myself to speak.

"It's just that everybody feels sorry for a widow."

That's one of the things I hate about it, in addition to all those other things....

"But no one feels sorry for a divorcee," she says, voice lowered. "Everybody looks at me differently."

As if she's crazy for leaving such a good guy. Yeah, I can understand that. But she deserves to be happy, and if she's sure she can't be with Keith, then she needs to leave him.

I clear my throat before advising her, "Don't worry about how everyone looks at you."

"How do you do that?" she asks.

It's not unusual for her to seek my advice despite her being the oldest. Emma does, too. I'd like to think it's because they've always thought I had it together. But maybe it's just because I remind them the most of Mom.

"How do you *not* care?" she clarifies.

"I was married to Rob for seventeen years. The man was not exactly shy and retiring." He was the life of every party. Heck, he could make standing in line at the bank a party. The silly little games he'd concoct to pass the time, his own perverse versions of I Spy—I spy a toupee, a panty line....

"Seriously, Pam, you can't worry about what other people think."

"Good advice," Mom says, as she comes up behind

us. She puts an arm around each of us. "What are my oldest and youngest talking about?"

Pam shoots me a glance. "Nothing."

Oh, God, when is she going to tell her about filing? But I, unlike the rest of town, can understand her worrying about what Mom thinks. And after Rachael's reaction, maybe Pam doesn't dare risk it, since Mom is her landlord.

"Doesn't sound like nothing," Mom says, her blue eyes watchful. Even though she's been working the room, she hasn't missed a thing going on with her kids. She's always been like that, probably since the day we were born.

I need to know how she does that, so I can always know what's going on with *my* kids. I'm afraid that if they stay as angry as they are, they're going to act out even more than they have.

I already have another meeting scheduled with the principal for later this afternoon. Maybe he's now able to prove that it's Robbie behind the pranks. Or maybe, despite my driving my son to and from school, he's found a way to skip class again.

Things aren't any better with Claire, either. I got some notes from teachers about her back-talking. Who can *I* send a note to about that? I wonder. And Claire's gusty sighs—who can I complain to about those?

Pam's tugging at my arm, but I haven't heard a word she's said.

"What?"

"Mom thinks it's a good idea, too. So will you do it?"

"Do what?"

"Work here for me while I go on a little trip. I really need a break."

What about what I need? I tap the paperwork on the counter. "I already work here."

Pam shakes her head. "Not hiding out in the back." She's one to talk. "Really working. Waiting tables with Mom."

My mother squeezes my shoulders, and I realize what I need might be right here. Working with her, I might actually get a chance to talk to her, really talk to her. She's always so busy with this place during the day and stuff at her condo complex at night.

Then the waitress, a woman not much younger than Mom, catches my attention as she glides past with a tray overloaded with thick slices of chocolate cake, frosting oozing over the sides of the plates.

"I don't know…." I respond.

I glance down at the counter, where the crumbs of a slice of carrot cake sit next to my cooling cup of tea. Actually, I do know. "That *wouldn't* be a good idea."

"Why not?" Pam asks, following my gaze to where Nina's delivering the cake.

"It's your fault. You're the one who always calls me a hypocrite. How can I feed people this stuff feeling the way I do? And we all know I'm no baker."

Mom chuckles. "That's true."

"So make salads," Pam says, as if it's all so simple.

"I wouldn't mind adding some to the menu," Mom admits, patting her trim waist. "Actually, I think it's an idea well past its time. You're no baker, but you do make a mean salad, Holly."

Yes, I do. Too bad Rob hadn't stuck with eating those. "I'm busy right now, though," I hedge, "with the kids."

"We don't open until after school starts and we close before it's out. I don't see how that's a problem," Mom points out, watching me again.

She knows I'm having problems with the kids that I haven't solved with finding Robbie. Do I have dark circles beneath my eyes from all the sleepless nights? I can't blame those all on the kids, though. It hasn't been easy to sleep in that big bed alone, in the silence.

"Claire's birthday is coming up," I remind her. "I want to throw her a big party." When I think about it, I'm not sure she has any friends left to invite. Nobody has called the house for her.

Robbie gets more calls, ones during which he whispers into the phone so I can't overhear his conversation. But I can't give Robbie all my attention. Even though she'd be the last to admit it, Claire needs me, too.

"It's her last year before becoming a teenager." The thought tightens my chest so that I have to breathe harder for a moment. I can't believe she's growing up so fast, and growing further and further away from me with each year. "I want to do something special for her."

Mom squeezes my shoulder. "You will, honey. And I'll help you."

"Then I'll help *you*," I agree.

Maybe working here with Mom will be *my* break— my breakthrough on how to reach my children. Hopefully, Mom can help me figure out more than how to make Claire's twelfth birthday special.

Then the bell above the door dings, and my attention is drawn to the entrance. Wide shoulders in a blue uniform fill the doorway. Suddenly I realize I haven't made the smartest decision. Waiting on customers means waiting on *him*. It's not just that I owe him an apology that irritates me when it comes to Deputy Westmoreland.

He's calm. Unshakable. He's probably only a few years older than me, so it's not as if he gained wisdom through advanced age. But he has it together.

And I do not.

"How are you doing?" I ask Keith as I open the door at the first brush of his knuckles against the wood. I've been watching for him to cross the street, worried that he might back out of my dinner invitation. He pauses outside, his jaw tense, as if he's wary of taking a step across the threshold, so I grab his arm and pull him inside.

"Holly!" A laugh bubbles out of him, shattering his solemn expression with a grin.

"You shouldn't have knocked," I scold him, missing those days when he, Pam, Rob and I had gone freely into each other's homes. But so much has changed since then....

"I really appreciate your inviting me, Holly," he says, all awkward and stilted, talking as if we're mere acquaintances and not family. Not that Keith's ever been all that relaxed of a guy. Even on his own time, he looks the part of a banker in his pressed khakis and polo shirt.

But his clothes are a little loose, his face a bit gaunt. Guilt flashes through me—I should have invited him for dinner sooner. "You don't need an invitation, Keith," I insist, "you're welcome anytime."

He smiles again, but it doesn't reach his solemn eyes. "I wasn't sure...."

"I know Pam filed," I admit, realizing she has him sworn to such secrecy that he doesn't dare mention it first. "She's my sister, and I love her, but I think she's crazy."

His smile widens, creasing his cheeks à la Clint Eastwood. He's better looking now than when Pam married him twenty-five years ago, and back then, he'd been the object of my first teenage crush. I can't imagine what she's thinking.

"Holly," he says with a self-deprecating chuckle, "I appreciate the sentiment, but Pam's not crazy. Just unhappy. I've known it for a long time. And as hard as I tried—as we both tried—I've finally accepted that *I* can't make her happy."

So he hadn't been surprised by the separation or her filing. That's good to know, for it makes me a little less irritated with Pam.

"I'm sorry," I say, wincing as I hear that tone in my voice, that pitying one I hate so much when people use it to address me.

He brushes off my concern, even as he blushes. "I'll be fine. Eventually. You know…."

I know that it hurts. And that it'll take time. And I keep waiting for it to get better.

His flush deepens and he starts stammering, "Not—not that I mean to compare my situation to yours. I know they're completely different—"

I wave off his concern. "They both hurt. You need your friends around you." Not deserting you because they don't know what to say. "Remember that I'm your friend, Keith. You can talk to me."

He opens his mouth to say something just as my children erupt from their bedrooms, the music from their respective stereos blaring out the open doors behind them. The floorboards nearly vibrate with the dueling beats. That's undoubtedly why they didn't hear me when I shouted out that Keith was here when I saw him crossing the road from his drive to mine. At least that's the excuse they give me anytime they don't do what I want.

"Mom, I'm hungry," Robbie yells above his own music. "When's Uncle Keith getting here?"

"He's here," I point out, drawing Keith deeper into our home. "Come say hello."

Claire murmurs a quick greeting in a rare moment of shyness from her; I wonder if she's inherited the crush I once had on him. She's almost the age I was when Pam first introduced him to our family. Then she flops onto the couch with such force that it moves despite her slight weight.

Robbie approaches with even more shyness, in shades of his old self. "Thanks for looking for me that night, Uncle Keith. I'm sorry I wasted your time like that."

"It wasn't a waste of my time," Keith swears, and his adamant tone suggests he really means it. "And you already apologized. You really don't need to, Robbie."

He apologized to Keith and Troy and his cousin Dylan, Emma's son who's a senior this year, the night he ran away. But that evening, since I'd been just about twisting his arm to do it, Robbie hadn't meant it. I'm not sure he does tonight, but his eyes, behind his thick lenses, are soft with sympathy. We all feel sorry for Keith. With Pam gone and Rachael on the other side of the state, he's completely alone. We, at least, have each other.

"Sit down," I tell Keith, as I head toward the kitchen. "I have to finish the salad, then we'll eat." As I rip up lettuce, I twist my neck around to stare into the great room. It's too quiet. I want lively conversation, but there's none of that going on.

Keith is sitting on the couch between Robbie and Claire, which is probably saving Robbie's ribs. Instead of talking, all three are staring at the news, and the volume is so low that I can't hear from the kitchen what the anchor people are saying. I can understand my family's awkwardness. It's strange for just the four of us to be together…without Rob here. Or Pam, who's out of town.

I thought she was just heading up north for a weekend. Instead she booked a two-week Bahamas cruise. That's not just a break, that's really running away. Good thing Robbie never goes to Pam for advice.

I wish he'd go to Keith, who was good friends with Rob. I hope the same can be true for them. Robbie needs some male influence in his life, at least that's what the principal told me at our meeting last week. He said that Robbie dropped the silly pranks and has started hanging with the wrong kind of crowd; I suspect he means a certain stepcousin.

Then, as he's also principal of the middle school, Mr. Van Otten talked about Claire, too. She's becoming the wrong kind of crowd all by herself, the back-talking, pushing-around-other-kids kind of crowd. She almost got suspended over fighting with Heather; apparently the girl thinks it's funny to make Claire mad now. It certainly doesn't take much effort. So my daughter is becoming a hotheaded bully, my son a delinquent.

And I'm a crazy woman who talks to a hula girl lamp. Yes, it's good that I'm working with Mom now. But something—maybe pride—holds me back from sharing everything with her.

She never had these problems after Dad died. Of course, when she became a widow, her children were full-grown, not teenagers. I really can't use her experience as a guidebook anymore. I have to find my own way. There's no rule that I have to do it alone, though.

"Robbie, why don't you show Uncle Keith your new computer game?" I ask. It's something he and Rob would have played for hours and I'd have had to drag them from the den for dinner. I ignore the scents of chicken mixed with garlic and rosemary drifting from the oven. It's ready and will dry out if I leave it in there, but Robbie making a connection to a male role model will be worth a little extra chewing.

Robbie looks to his uncle. "It's really new. Great graphics."

"I didn't bring my glasses," Keith says, then sighs. "I probably left them at work. I don't remember much of anything anymore." No matter how fine he claims to be with it, Pam has turned his world upside down.

Maybe this cruise will give Pam some clarity and she'll figure out how to be happy *with* Keith instead of without. But I remember her conversation from the last time we walked, and I'm not holding my breath. I won't hold my breath until lively conversation starts up in the great room, either; I'd pass out for sure.

"Dad might've had some glasses downstairs, but I'm sure Mom gave them away," Claire says, then resentfully adds, "like everything else."

"Claire, set the table." I reward her for her sarcasm. It's better than the detentions her teachers are starting to give her. She's worn out their sympathy for her. Besides plotting against me, she and her brother have something else they can do together after school.

She blows out some hot air, then stomps into the dining room. Keith's squirming on the couch, clearly struggling with the tension in our home. Maybe he'll find out being alone isn't so bad.

At the very least, I intend to get a healthy meal in him. I shudder to think what he's been feeding himself since Pam left. From the way his clothes are hanging on him, I doubt it's been Kitty Cupcakes. Smiley has yet to restock them—he probably doesn't dare carry them in his store anymore.

Our dinner is strained and awkward. Keith eats and flees. I can't say I blame him. It's not much fun around here anymore. And it's probably hard for him to be here without Rob.

Robbie is downstairs, playing that game I bribed him with. Our agreement is that he can only keep it with good behavior. Hopefully, he'll stick to it.

I'm helping Claire finish up her chore of dishes. Although, honestly, it's probably more like she's helping me as she halfheartedly dries the square stoneware plates with stripes of orange, red and yellow—my last Christmas present from Rob, which I will never trust to the dishwasher.

"So," I say, trying to sound all casual. "Someone has a birthday coming up."

She doesn't answer. Has she forgotten her own special day?

"Whatever," she finally says, showing me how unspecial it is to her.

"Your last preteen year," I tease her.

She shrugs. "I think that means more to you than it does to me."

Obviously.

"What kind of party do you want?" I ask. "I was

thinking about renting a room in Grand Rapids in a hotel with a big pool. You could invite—"

"Nobody. I don't want a stupid party. I'm not a little girl anymore. Jeez, Mom."

Now I've done it. She's all offended, her jaw taut, her face red.

"Okay, just family then."

"What family? Our family's all screwed up now."

The awkwardness of the evening was apparently not lost on Claire. *Thanks, Pam.* Couldn't she have waited a little longer before turning our family upside down again? A death, a divorce, it's too much for one year. We still aren't entirely recovered from losing my dad yet, and that's been six years.

"Do you think I'll forget him?" she asks quietly.

"Uncle Keith? He'll still be around. In fact, I think Aunt Pam's going to let him have the house." She couldn't wait to get off the farm.

"I'm not talking about *him*," she says, her voice muffled as she turns away from me.

Rob. For just a moment my heart lurches as her fear becomes mine. Could she forget him? She's so young, too young to lose the most important man in her life.

"Your father? Of course you'll remember him," I say, assuring myself as much as her. I quickly dry my hands on the front of my shirt. But when I put them on her thin shoulders, she shrugs them off.

Maybe I should do something Rob would have done, like tickle her until she giggles. He used to do that all the time, and not just to her and Robbie, but to me, too. But this doesn't feel like a time to giggle. Tears are burning my eyes, and even though she won't face me, I can tell she's blinking hers away.

Trying to be strong. Trying to be cool. She's not the little girl who used to love to cuddle. Even before Rob died, she hadn't been that girl for a while. The one who would curl up on your lap like a cat the minute you sat down. *That* sweet little girl I had understood so well; I don't know this stranger she's become. I don't know how to comfort her even if she'd let me.

All I can manage is a helpless "Claire…"

Her shoulders are shaking along with her voice when she says, "I don't remember Grandpa."

"Ah, honey." I blink hard, too, to clear my eyes. "You were five when he died, but you probably remember more than you think. He was a quiet man." So unlike her father. "He loved you very much." He had such a big heart, like Emma. "He always took you down to the barns to see the calves when they were first born."

"Okay…" she says, shooting me a glance over her shoulder. Her eyes are damp. "I remember the baby cows."

She would. She loves animals as much as Mrs. Diller loves her flowers. Suddenly I know what I have to get her for her birthday.

"You were only five and you remember that," I point out. "You have so many more memories of your father that there's no way you can forget him."

"How do you know?" she asks, her mouth twisted into that petulant pout. "You were old when your dad died."

Early thirties is old? What I wouldn't give to be *that old* again. Sure, I'd lost my dad and thought that was the worst thing that could ever happen to me. If only I'd known back then what I do now....

I would have kicked Kitty's ass a long time ago.

More important than the slight on my age, I detect that note of resentment in her voice again. Because I had my dad longer than she had hers?

In my continuing effort to bridge the distance between us, I'm about to apologize for this when she picks up a plate and...drops it. Against the ceramic tile floor, it breaks apart into jagged shards of orange, red and yellow.

This isn't an accident; she wasn't drying it. She'd already tossed the towel down on the counter. I'm not sure what it is—a diversion so we stop talking about what's making her uncomfortable...or an act of vengeance?

"Claire!"

She turns to me, her mouth a hard, bitter line while her eyes are still bright with the tears she's fighting so hard. "What? You're going to yell at me now?"

She acts as if that's all I do, but I don't think I yell

nearly enough. She knows how much these plates mean to me, and if she broke it on purpose, she did it to hurt me. To take something away from me, like she feels I took so much away from her.

What? Her father's clothes? They were in my closet, and neither she nor her brother would ever wear them. His business? It would be at least ten years before either of them could take it over.

It's not as if I've packed pictures away and obliterated every trace of their father. Rob was always the one behind the camera, taking pictures of us. He'd always threatened that his ugly mug would break the camera if he were in front of it. I think he was unnecessarily self-conscious about his size. I'd thought he was perfect.

So had his children. I know they're hurting. But I'm hurting, as well, and I'm getting sick of feeling guilty for something I haven't done.

I think now about going downstairs, about ripping Rob's corny fishing-tackle wallpaper off the den walls. He never went fishing so I'm not sure why he wanted that paper, or the goofy fishing knickknacks, except to irritate me. I should throw all of that away and make that room mine. He can't use it anymore and I need it.

But I'm trying to be sensitive to what my children need. I'm trying to be here for them, the way Rob would have been. So I fight the anger surging up inside me.

And I promise my hateful young daughter, "You won't forget your dad, Claire."

I think she's disappointed that I don't fight because her dark eyes widen and her mouth falls open, as shocked as if I'd slapped her. Then she runs past me to her room, slamming the door so hard that it feels as if the house shakes.

I drop to my knees beside the shards, grabbing them in my hands, uncaring that they're digging into my palms. That I'm bleeding. I've been bleeding inside for a long time already.

STAGE 7

"So how's the party planning going?" Mom asks, as we share the morning setup at The Tearoom.

I jam some sugar packets into the back of a cow-shaped porcelain container with such force that one crumples. "Dead in the water. She's too old for a party."

"She's still getting a family one," Mom insists.

I don't tell her what Claire said about our family even though I know now that she wasn't talking about Keith and Pam. Our family is screwed up because Rob's gone. The child's not wrong.

"Sure, Mom," I hasten to agree. "We'll have cake and ice cream on Sunday."

Mom wrinkles her nose. "She's not a little girl anymore, honey."

"Where have I heard that before?" I ask, pretending to consider the rhetorical question.

Mom laughs. "You've heard it but do you understand it?"

"What? Should I take her to a Grateful Dead concert instead of getting her a cake?"

"Holly," Mom says, fighting a smile. "I doubt she knows who the Grateful Dead are. I'm not sure I know."

Neither do I, but I recognize their name more than any of the bands whose posters decorate her walls, along with the kittens.

"Sure, Mom, I know she's growing up." She's probably already a cup-size ahead of me. Note to self: buy her more bras. "But that doesn't mean I have to accept it."

Mom sighs. "Yeah, I went that route with Pam. Wouldn't recommend it. She lives here and works with me, but we're still not close."

Not like Mom and I are. A victory in thirty-eight years of sibling rivalry warms my heart.

"For instance, she hasn't told me yet that she's filed for divorce." Her eyes narrow. "And neither have you."

All that warmth evaporates under her disapproval. "Mom, it wasn't my place to tell you."

She snorts. "That's never stopped you before." I'm about to protest when she laughs. "Just kidding, sweetheart. I know it wasn't your place."

"So how'd you find out? The mayor?"

"Keith, actually. He stopped by before you got here, on his way to work." Before she opens.

But he's family, not a customer. And no matter what a divorce decree says, I know Mom feels as I do, that he'll always be family. And good for him that he disobeyed Pam's vow of silence. Perhaps he's finally standing up for himself.

Mom says, "He comes by every day, gets a cup of coffee and a piece of carrot cake before work."

Maybe that's why Pam usually hides out in the back when she's here. I actually thought about doing that myself the first couple of days I filled in for her. I've had about as much pity and sympathy as I can stand, but I think it's been long enough that people have begun to forget.

Maybe Claire is right to worry.

The only thing I'm getting from the customers is grief when the water isn't hot enough to steep the tea. And the salads—I took a lot of flack over them, until people tried them.

I lift my chin with a little pride. Now they order them without any of my arm-twisting.

I gather up the extra sugar packets and carry the box behind the counter, where Mom is checking the pots. The coffee is brewing, the hot water rumbling in the machine before rich brown liquid streams into each glass carafe.

"He said you fed him last night," Mom says.

I nod. "I'm worried about him."

"You worry about a lot of people," she says. "Your kids, Keith, Pam…"

"So do you," I remind her. "Me, Emma, Pam, all of

your grandkids." I sweep an arm around the empty dining room. "And probably every customer who walks through the door."

Her smile is wan, as if she's forcing it. "Okay, you've made your point. I shouldn't be throwing stones."

Then she yawns and rubs her hand across her drooping eyes. I don't think she has the energy for any stone-throwing.

"Late night?" I tease.

"Getting old," she claims with a self-deprecating chuckle.

I don't laugh with her. The lines are deep around her eyes and mouth. Today, for the first time, I notice that my mother *is* getting old. And I add another person to my worry-about list.

She's sixty-seven, past the retirement age. Maybe The Tearoom is too much for her. If I could trust the kids to actually get on the bus, I'd come in earlier to help her. But Pam will be back soon, so she can do that.

Or maybe Mom should consider retirement. She should be in a different place, emotionally, now than she was when Dad first died. It hasn't been a year with Rob and already I'm in a different place.

I may have just sold one business, but I would consider buying another…*this one*, if my mother ever decided to sell. To my surprise, I enjoy working here. I have more contact with the public than in Rob's old business or with my bookkeeping sideline. And because Stanville is so small, I know everyone who walks through the door. Every day is a bit like a class reunion or a wedding.

But I know how much this place once meant to my mother and still might. I can't risk asking because she loves me so much, she might actually sell it to me even though she doesn't want to part with it.

The minute we flip the Open sign, customers start streaming in. There's a diner in town and a handful of fast-food restaurants, even a couple of grills, but my mother has the most regulars. The mayor hangs out here, using it as his second office, which, ironically, is only open the same limited number of hours. Groups of retired men meet here every day, and ladies' clubs. They come as much for my mother's charm as the tea, coffee, cake or, now, salad.

To open any kind of similar business in Stanville would put me in direct competition with my mother. And she would kick my ass. No, if I want a tearoom of my own, I'd have to move, and I already promised the kids I wouldn't.

As I flit around the restaurant, refilling teapots and coffee cups, I absorb the cheerful ambiance of warm chatter and the rich aromas of coffee and cinnamon. Pam's coming home soon, and she'll want her job back.

I know Mom won't fire me, but after owning a

business with Rob, I doubt I will stay satisfied with my part-time work at home. Then I remind myself that the only thing I really intended to work on since selling Rob's business was my relationship with my children.

And I suspect that's going to be a full-time job.

"So you had Keith over for dinner last night," Emma remarks, as we walk in perfect rhythm. Even the gravel crunching beneath the rubber soles of our tennis shoes is in harmony. "How's he doing?"

"Not good," I say.

"I've been meaning to have him over," she says, her pace slowing a bit. "But there's so much tension in my house...."

And there isn't in mine?

She should have been at dinner. Then I think about what she's just said. She and Troy may have some different ideas about how to parent, but they're very much in love. Like Rob, Troy brings his wife flowers at least once a week. Doesn't hurt that he works next door to a florist, but it's the thought, not the convenience, that counts. They also have a standing date every Friday night, their much-needed time away from their crazy blended household.

"What's going on, Emma?" I ask, remembering she'd been about to mention something last time we walked. This time there is no Pam running up to interrupt us. Emma stops walking entirely, as if she's too tired to take another step. "Troy's ex is back."

Like Emma's husband, the woman had abandoned Troy and her kids. That was one of the reasons why Emma had fallen for him: they had so much in common. She'd also felt sorry for him and his children, and she can't help but mother everyone even when she's agreed not to.

"You're not jealous…."

She shakes her head. "No, I know Troy loves me."

"But still, this is his ex. Are you okay?" I ask, scrutinizing her face. Her expressive eyes are bruised with dark circles and stress. Lines also rim her mouth.

She shrugs. "It's not about me. I'm just worried about the kids. She hurt them so bad when she left the first time. If she does it again…"

Jason might skip juvie and go straight to prison. I know I certainly have my concerns about him and his influence on Robbie, but I'm not entirely lacking in sympathy for him—the kid's had a rough time of it. He, and his sister, Melissa, can't take any more.

"Just because she's back doesn't mean she gets to see the kids again. No judge will enforce that after the way she abandoned them."

"Troy has already let her see them."

Troy. Not Emma. I can tell from the pain in her shaky voice this was not her idea.

"Emma…"

"He says she's their mother. They have a right to see her."

"So have they?"

"Just Melissa. Jason doesn't want to."

"Good for Jason."

"But Troy thinks he should, that it will help him get over this rough phase."

I sigh, knowing that I can't offer anything but support. If Troy won't listen to Emma, it certainly doesn't matter what I think. And heck, these are his kids, he knows them best; maybe he's right.

"Well, hey, if she helps him, let me know. She can start seeing Robbie and Claire, too."

A laugh bubbles out of Emma, sounding more like a hiccupping sob. "I didn't mean to dump this on you," she says, "when you already have so much going on."

"Really I don't."

I'm glad to be working with Mom at The Tearoom. I can even justify serving cake, since we're starting to sell an equal amount of salads and fruit plates. It all evens out in the end.

"The kids are busy," I say, starting to realize they are not a full-time job. "Claire has piano. Robbie is taking online computer courses. They both have detention."

"What do *you* have?" she asks.

"I'm working—"

"I don't mean *work*." She uses *that* tone. I expected this conversation coming from Pam someday, not my more sensible sister.

I sigh. "Emma…"

"So you know where I'm going with this," she surmises. "Well, then…"

I start walking again, hoping to outdistance her and myself from this conversation. "I'm not ready."

"Before you know it, it'll be a year."

"Not for another five months."

Actually four months, three weeks and six days. I could name the hours, minutes and seconds, too, if I were wearing a watch. But I'm not.

"It's been long enough, Holly. People would understand."

People might. But I wouldn't.

"Hey, it's been six years for Mom, and she hasn't started dating yet." I like that part of her widow guidebook best, since I can follow that.

"Mom's almost seventy."

Not that anyone would guess that from looking at her. Usually. Today she'd looked every bit her age. I think about asking her about selling The Tearoom.

"So," Emma says, "Troy might know someone single we could set you up with. I'll ask him—"

"To keep his wife out of my business," I interrupt, my tone teasing, while I'm quite serious. "Let's talk about how stupid Pam's being." That's a topic we can usually agree on.

She laughs. "Don't sidetrack me."

The sudden approach of a car does just that, though, as we move to the shoulder of the road. It roars past, kicking up a far bigger cloud of dust and dry leaves than Pam had the day she ran to catch us. Through watery eyes, I catch a glimpse of the heavily pierced driver. "That was Jason!"

She nods, and once again her expressive eyes are full of stress. "Yes."

"But…" I don't bother pointing out that Troy would not buy *her* daughter a car, and she needs to drive to school in Grand Rapids every day. That was why I'd loaned Sally the Beetle. She's a good girl. When Emma was alone, Sally helped out with her younger brothers while Emma worked as a teller at the bank Keith manages; she still works there, part-time. And she would have used that money to buy Sally a car, but I offered Rob's instead. It's not as though he was using it.

Emma shrugs again. "Troy bought him the car so Jason could drive to town to see his mother whenever he wants."

"But he doesn't want to." All Troy's bribe did was cause more tension in Emma's house.

She sighs. "I don't want to talk about it anymore."

I catch her hand as she swings it at her side, and squeeze. "But you know that you can, right?"

She turns toward me, eyes wide with the question she doesn't ask.

"You know you can talk to me about anything," I clarify.

She laughs. "It's funny how Pam and I come to you for advice, and you're the baby."

I laugh now. "I'm hardly a baby anymore."

And I wish it wasn't just my sisters who sought my counsel. Too bad my kids don't feel they can trust me with their burdens, such as why Robbie's skipping and Claire's alienating all her friends.

"No, you're not. You're a widow now." She says it with *that* tone. Too much respect for pity, but there's an unspoken *poor Holly* in there.

As I've told Pam before, I didn't choose this, but I'm damn well going to deal with it. "Yes."

"After my divorce, I never thought I'd get involved again," Emma murmurs. "I didn't think it was worth it to put myself out there and risk getting hurt."

Her honesty softens my heart. "Em…"

"But then *someone* pestered me to date again."

That was Rob, not me. He loved playing matchmaker, probably would have dressed up like Cupid if I'd let him. Rob met Troy when he put the computer system in his service shop, and he'd thought Troy and

Emma had a lot in common. And Rob hadn't wanted Emma to be alone. He'd wanted her to be happy, like we were.

Emma continues, "And I fell in love, harder than I'd ever been before. Sure, it's crazy, but it's worth it, Holly."

I have my doubts, but I'm sensitive this once and don't voice them. Love someone more than Rob? Not possible. "Not going to happen, Em," I tell her.

Not the dating. Definitely not the falling in love again. I suspect I'm like a wolf or a crane, whichever has one mate for life. Rob was mine. No matter how much dating I would do, I could never find another man like him.

"You're too young to be alone, Holly."

"I'm not alone. I have the kids." When they talk to me. "And I'm thinking about getting a kitten. Your mama cat have any more?"

"That slut?" she laughs. "Yeah, she's got a litter just about ready to wean. But I thought you didn't want animals in the house?"

She remembers that I sent the kids back with the one Claire stole from her barn, and she remembers when it happened. I can tell by the moisture she's blinking away. Emma with her big, soft heart. No wonder Troy and his kids walk over her.

I swallow a sigh. "Yeah, well, I've changed my mind."

The house isn't as important to me as it once was. I

won't mind shredded drapes and soiled carpet if it brings a smile to Claire's face.

"I need one for a birthday present in a couple of days. Will they be weaned by then?"

Emma takes a playful swing at my arm. "The cat's not to keep *you* company. It's for Claire."

"She can use the company," I say. Since she won't talk to any person anymore, maybe she'll talk to the cat.

"Claire's not the only one who can use the company," Emma says, a teasing glint twinkling in her eyes. "You really need to think about dating."

I would laugh, but it's much too sad. I can't tell her what I really think about dating. Later, in my bedroom, I tell the lamp. "I'd rather be alone than live like she does."

It smiles in agreement.

If I don't want to stay single, I have to risk the life Emma leads now. The life of *my* kids, *his* kids and, damn it, I'm young enough that we could even have *our* kids. Claire and Robbie are pissed at me now; how would they handle a baby brother or sister? I imagine them pulling late-night feedings and diaper duty, and start laughing. The lamp sways back and forth, almost as if the hula girl is laughing with me.

Or maybe *at* me. At this predicament Rob has left me in. With the kids. With being single at thirty-eight. Emma is right—I am young. Too young to completely give up the physical side of a relationship. But with Rob it had been making love, with anyone else it would be just sex.

"So what's bothering you?" Mom asks. "Have you served more cake than fruit and salad today?"

I can't tell her I'm worried about Emma because then she'll worry, too, and she's already worried enough about me the past several months. Despite her energy, I can see her age again today. It shows in the pronounced cords of her neck and the dark blue veins running across the backs of her hands. She places one of her hands over mine as I'm wiping the counter.

"Holly?"

"How did you handle it, Mom?" I ask.

I've asked her so many questions since Rob died. But not this one. I don't know *how* to ask.

"What? How did I handle what?"

I shake my head. "Forget it."

I think she already has. She lets me pull away and continue wiping, for a moment. The next she's spinning me into the kitchen, and as I twirl in her arms, past stainless steel appliances and counters, I flash to Rob spinning me around the kitchen of our house the same way.

There was no slipping past Rob without a waltz or a dip. With all his energy, he'd really had to consume the calories to weigh what he had. *Metabolism problem, my ass, Rob.*

As the swinging door of the kitchen closes behind us, Mom puts her thumb and finger on my chin, lifting it so that my gaze meets hers. I remember all the times she'd done that to extract one of Pam's or Emma's secrets from me. I always caved.

I'm tempted to even now.

I can get her to forget my vague question if I tell her about Emma and the problems with Troy and his ex. But despite what Pam thinks, I'm not a tattletale anymore.

"How did I handle what?" she asks again. Although those fingers are gentle, her grasp on my chin is firm.

I can be vague no more. I sigh. "All the pushing."

"What pushing?"

To be honest, there's only been Emma, but I figure that's just because Pam's out of town. When she returns next week, she'll be pushing, too.

"The pushing to…"

I can't even say it; the word makes me gag as if I'm bingeing on Kitty Cupcakes. Except it wouldn't mean cheating on a diet, it would mean cheating on *Rob*.

"To?" she asks, lifting my chin a little higher, so that I can't avoid her scrutiny or her question.

So, like ripping off a Band-Aid, I hurl it out there. "Date."

"Someone's urging you to date?" She studies my face. "Has someone asked you out?"

I laugh because it's ridiculous. I shouldn't have given Emma's insistence any thought. "No," I admit. "Nobody has asked me out."

And no one probably will. I'm a widow with two resentful kids. It's not as if Stanville is exactly teeming with eligible men.

Even if someone were fool enough to ask me, I would have to say no. For so many reasons. The resentful kids being number one. I don't want Claire breaking any more of my dishes, or Robbie running away again.

I glance down at my hands, at the diamond engagement and wedding rings melded into a thick band around my finger. The real reason I'd have to say no is that I'm still married. My husband may be dead, but I'm still married.

I say it again. "Nobody's asked me out."

Mom doesn't laugh at me, but I can see the amusement in her blue eyes. "Then don't go looking for trouble, Holly."

My father said the same words to her several times, whenever she'd been pushing for the secrets Emma and Pam kept from her while they were growing up. But it applies to this situation, too. Good advice. She always gives it.

"Thanks, Mom." For pointing out the obvious. "Of course *you* would know how to handle it."

"Who says I have?" She tosses the words over her

shoulder as she waltzes back out the door to the dining room, and I wonder what she means. That no one has asked her out in the last six years, or something else....

I follow her to find out, but before I can so much as lift a brow, she's putting the handle of a coffeepot in my hand. "Time for refills," she says. "You get the counter. I'll handle the rest."

Her eyes are still shining. Then I see she's heading toward Smiley, and I'm happy to stay behind the counter...until I glance along it and see who's sitting a few stools down. "Deputy Westmoreland."

Pam must enjoy waiting on him, since she thinks he's so attractive. He's probably only a few years younger than she is—maybe she can ask him out once her divorce is final. I wish I'd known how long she was going to be gone. Not that I don't love working here. Usually.

I would have made Pam reschedule her trip because she's going to miss Claire's birthday party. But I can't let Claire's special day pass without any fanfare just to wait until her aunt Pam comes back.

"Mrs. DeJong." He says my name just as awkwardly as I say his. Then he covers his cup with his hand as I brandish the pot across the counter.

For just a second, I consider pouring anyway. Every time I see him I struggle with this strange mixture of anger and embarrassment, and the anger usually wins.

"Decaf, please," he says.

I grab the orange handle for that pot and hold it so tightly my fingers start to ache. He moves his hand and I fill his cup, not so full that it overflows. I have restraint. Today.

"Thanks."

I nod.

But before I can walk away, he stops me. "Mrs. DeJong…"

"Holly." It slips out. I don't intend to offer him the use of my first name, but when you've pummeled and sobbed all over a man, it seems strange *not* to be on a first-name basis with him.

"Holly," he says.

I must be standing under an air vent because for some reason I shiver. But why would Mom have the air on this late in October?

I glance over to her. She's leaning over Smiley; they're talking close. It looks pretty intense. I hope their conversation isn't about me.

"Holly," the deputy repeats.

This time I suppress the shiver.

"I need to talk to you," he adds.

Suddenly I'm freezing. They aren't the same words he used that night, they're not even close. But for some reason they remind me of those.

I shake my head. "I can't do this right now. It's busy…."

I start backing toward the kitchen.

He's watching me, the way he watched me that night, as if I'm going to fall apart and he needs to know how to put me back together after it happens.

Except he didn't put me back together.

I did.

STAGE 8

Over the twelve burning candles on her cake, Claire gives me *that* look. The one every adolescent girl develops that eloquently expresses her resentment of all things, but most especially her mother. What we need right now is one of her huffy breaths to accompany it so that she blows out those candles.

To spite me, she's probably going to let all the wax melt onto the cake I spent the afternoon baking and decorating. Baking is so not my thing.

"Don't spit on it," Robbie says threateningly, or as threatening as an ever-changing voice can be when it inexplicably goes up an octave midsentence.

"Make a wish," my mother reminds her.

I'm a little worried when a suspicious gleam enters my daughter's eyes. Then she draws in a deep breath, puffing out her cheeks. She blows it back out in a big rush, extinguishing all the candles.

With satisfaction, Mom declares, "Your wish will come true now."

That worries me.

It's only the four of us. Even though I didn't honor her wish for no party, I kept it small. No aunts, uncles or cousins. Just Robbie, Mom and me. From Claire's stare, I can tell she thinks that's too many. And the cake is too much. Hopefully the presents will make her happy because these days it seems that nothing else does.

I understand that only too well.

"Open mine first," Robbie says, sliding the thin, square package toward her.

I smile, amused that he's taking so much credit for it when I'd had to give him the money and nearly force him to pick out something. Apparently, it's *uncool* to buy a gift for your sister.

And lately Robbie's all about cool. That's probably why he skips school. Shopping for Claire wound up being more like shopping for him, which reminds me of the way Claire shops for others, too. He's wearing the ripped jeans with the paint spatters we bought. I'm not sure why he couldn't have taken a pair of his old jeans and done this, but the new ones were on clearance, so I didn't quibble too much. In fact, I was happy he was finally interested in clothes.

Until now.

Now he's wearing a black T-shirt with some suspiciously satanic symbol on the front, although both he and Claire assured me it really belongs to some skater, a reality TV star. Through the belt loops of the jeans, he's strung a few chains that are clipped together with a padlock. I hope he knows where the key is in case he has to make a quick trip to the bathroom.

The chains weren't the only accessories he wanted. He tried wheedling me into letting him get piercings. I can't imagine where he would have gotten the idea for those. And again, I'm glad that no cousins are at Claire's party. I feel a little bad about not including Emma, but she understands almost-teenagers.

And Pam. If I'd had Emma here and not Pam… It wouldn't matter to Pam that she was out of town. I'm sure she'd still be mad.

"Did you get any of that goop on it?" Claire asks, before reaching for the gift from her brother.

She's referring to the product he put in his hair that has the dark strands standing on end. I know what look he's going for; I've seen it at my sister's house. But with his thick glasses and thin face, he looks more like a dark-haired Muppet than the badass he's shooting for. Claire has been quick to ridicule him about his new look.

I hope no one else has been, but I put nothing past my stepnephew. How else has he had such an influence on him?

"Just open it," Robbie says impatiently, ignoring her question.

Claire holds the thin package with two fingers, then wiggles it back and forth as if shaking the contents. "Gee, I wonder what this is. Really original...."

I hope she's a bit more appreciative when she opens it, but I can never be sure about her attitude or, apparently, Robbie's taste. Both are questionable.

Over the birthday girl's head, Mom shoots me an encouraging smile. If she hadn't guessed before, she now knows I'm struggling with these strangers with whom I share a home. These are not the children I've raised for fifteen and twelve years.

Claire finally tears the metallic paper off the CD. She doesn't say anything, which is actually a good thing lately.

"Do you like it?" I'm the one to ask.

I have no idea who the group is, but there was no parental advisory on it, unlike a few others Robbie tried to get me to buy. And the young men in the picture looked vaguely familiar, like maybe they were on one of the posters on her walls.

Instead of a thank-you, she just nods. I can tell it moves Robbie because he has to swallow before saying, "I'm going to burn a copy of it."

"What?" my mother asks.

I'm grateful for the years spent in the computer business, so that I know what he's talking about. "He's going to make a copy of it."

"Yeah, he bought it for himself," Claire says, tossing it down next to the cake.

"Well," my mother says, "I'm sure that's not what Robbie did. And I didn't buy this for myself, either." She hands her present to Claire.

"Thanks, Grandma," Claire says sweetly, before she even opens it. She spoils the effect, though, by the glare she shoots at her brother.

The box is small, and I'm worried that it's jewelry. I learned last Christmas never to buy Claire jewelry. Apparently, so has my mother, because there's a gift certificate to any store in the mall in Grand Rapids inside.

Inwardly I groan over another shopping trip. But I know my mother has done the right thing because Claire gives her a genuine thank-you and a quick hug.

Mom smiles. "I'm glad you like it. Myself, I hate the mall. Too crowded. I much prefer Smiley's."

Me, too. Even with his surveillance of me now, I'd rather shop there than travel to Grand Rapids with two feuding kids in the car. Alone, the trip wouldn't seem that long. With them along, it's never-ending.

Claire looks to me with just one arched brow, silently asking me where her gift is.

"I'll start cutting the cake," I say, suppressing a smile at her huffy breath of impatience. She may not have wanted the party, but she sure wants the presents. "Robbie, you can go get that box out of my bedroom."

He doesn't hesitate, obviously as excited about this gift as Claire will probably be. I'll hold off on adding ice cream to the slices of cake I'm doling onto dessert plates. I'm sure this gift will distract us all from eating for a while.

Claire doesn't say a word until Robbie walks out of my bedroom, his spindly arms wrapped tightly around the box he's carrying. "You didn't wrap it," Claire says, her tone accusatory.

She didn't want the cake, candles or party, but she wanted the fancy wrapping paper? I doubt I'll ever understand her again. Maybe she and I are destined to be like Mom and Pam.

"You can't wrap this gift," Robbie says, curiously defending me. "It'll kill—"

"Just let her open the box," I quickly interject, motioning for him to set it on the floor.

Reluctantly Claire leaves her place of honor and kneels on the carpet next to the box. Before she can peel back the flaps, a little mewl emanating from inside gives the gift away. I expect a smile from her, some reaction. She says nothing, but her hands are shaking as she opens it.

She doesn't reach for it. The kitten climbs out on its own, its little orange-striped head appearing over the side as its claws tear through the cardboard.

"It's so cute," my mother gushes, joining Claire beside the box. "Is this one of Emma's?"

Mom glances over her shoulder at me, but her eyes have more questions than about the origin of the kitten. Claire has still not said anything.

"Yes, the latest litter from her mama kitty."

"It's adorable," Mom says. "If I was home more, I'd get one for myself. It gets lonely living alone."

That's the first time she's ever admitted it. I make a mental note to pursue that when she and I have some private time, which isn't often. But right now, Claire is my main concern.

"What will you name it?" I ask her.

"It's a girl," Robbie says, stroking a finger over its little head as it hangs on to the top edge of the box. "How about Taz?"

"I'm not naming it," Claire says, rising from her knees and backing away from the box. "I'm not keeping it."

"Claire—"

She turns toward me now, angry, her eyes bright with unshed tears. "I don't want it!"

Before I can say anything, she rushes away from us, down the hall to her room. She slams the door hard.

"What a bitch," Robbie says.

I should scold him for calling his sister such a name. After all, we have the rule. But at the moment, I can't argue with him.

"What was that about?" I wonder aloud.

"You know Claire," Robbie says. "She's probably pissed that you didn't spend any money on her."

I really need to remind him of the rule and talk to him about his language. I'm not so naive as to believe teenagers don't swear. However, it's one thing for him to use it around his friends, another in front of his grandma....

My mother lifts the crying kitten and cradles it against her cheek. "I don't think Claire's problem with the kitten is that it was free," she says. She glances toward the hall, and I know without her saying more that she thinks the kitten isn't the only one crying right now.

"Robbie, can you bring it back to your aunt Emma's?" I ask.

The last thing I want to do is upset Claire more by keeping it, but I hear Robbie's gasp and see his eyes, wide and stricken, behind his lenses. And I know Claire is not the only one I've upset. I've reminded my son of the day he lost his father, too.

Oh, God, what was I thinking?

"I'll do it," my mother quickly offers, gathering up the box. I guess she knows it's best to remove every trace of it from our home.

I wish I'd known what was best. Tears sting my eyes, but I blink them back. Feeling bad isn't going to help fix my mistake.

"I'm going downstairs," Robbie says, his feet already hitting the steps.

"What about...cake?" The last word falls on deaf ears. Maybe it's better when they don't listen to me. At least I can't hurt them then.

But I can't take the easy way out of dealing with Claire. I need to talk to her.

"They'll eat it later," my mom says, as she heads toward the door.

"What about you? Don't you want some?" I appreciate her taking the kitten back, but I don't want her to leave. I don't feel like I can keep doing this alone.

She shakes her head. "Have to watch my figure, honey, or no one else will."

I manage a smile at her cute remark.

"You'll be fine," she assures me, just before the door closes behind her.

I'm not so sure. Maybe I should let Claire break more of my plates; it's not like anything could make me feel worse right now.

This time I knock before entering Claire's room. It gives her enough time to turn away from me, so that I don't see the tears I know she's shedding.

"I'm sorry," I tell her sincerely. "I thought you'd like a kitten. You've been asking for one for years."

She draws in a shaky breath, then asks, "How many times do I have to tell you I'm not a little girl anymore?"

Even knowing that there'll be other times, like when

she asks to go on her first date, or drive the car, or get married, I lie to her. "Never."

She's a smart girl. She knows I'm lying. I can see it in the doubt in her big, dark eyes as she turns back toward me. But she doesn't call me on it. She just nods with faint satisfaction.

"I'm going to get your brother," I tell her. "We'll go to the mall, spend Grandma's gift card and hit that Mexican restaurant you love so much for dinner."

I know it's wrong. Instead of addressing what I've done, instead of talking about that horrible day I've reminded them both of, I want to pretend everything's all right. It's Claire's birthday and I don't want to ruin it any more than I already have.

"Sound good?" I ask.

She nods again.

"Bring that CD Robbie got you."

"I don't think you'll like it, Mom." She scoffs, "It's not country."

Don't I know it. I don't remember when they switched from liking the music Rob and I liked to finding their own. Damn peer pressure.

"So broaden my horizons," I challenge her. And listening to a CD, no matter how bad, will be better than listening to them bickering during the long drive. "Bring some other CDs you like, too."

I probably should have brought her to a concert for

a birthday present. Not the Grateful Dead, but some group she knows and enjoys. I look at the walls and the posters for inspiration, and notice that the kittens are gone now.

She's right. She's not a little girl anymore. She hasn't been since her father died.

"It'll be better next year, Claire," I promise her as I leave her room to call Robbie up from the basement. This birthday, the first without her dad, was bound to be hard even without the mistakes I made.

I can only imagine how our first holidays without him will be.

Keith is over for dinner again. He's not nearly as depressed. In fact, he's almost hopeful. He probably knows Pam is coming home later tonight.

He remembered his glasses, and he and Robbie played the new game. I didn't have to drag them upstairs for dinner, though. Keith doesn't have that competitive edge that would drive Rob and Robbie to be at it for hours because neither would concede defeat.

I glimpse the disappointment in Robbie's eyes, magnified by those thick lenses. My intentions were pure, getting a male role model into Robbie's life, but I know that no one will replace his dad. So does he.

"Next time you'll have to come to my house," Keith says, as he helps Claire clear the table. "I'll barbecue."

He and Rob had barbecue-offs. Rob always won, probably due to his secret ingredient, brown sugar. Rob had once told me that if anything ever happened to him, I was to give his recipe to Keith. My hands are shaking as I open the antique brocade box and find the note card on which Rob had scrawled the recipe that, until the moment he wrote it down, he'd only kept in his head. Had he known?

The coroner told me there was evidence of other heart attacks, mild ones, that Rob had ignored…just as he'd ignored the diet I put him on. So yes, he probably had known, if only subconsciously. I hadn't. I've never been as shocked as I was that night, so much so that I lived in shock for six months *after* that night.

Robbie and Claire don't answer their uncle. They both mutter something about homework and head for their rooms. Homework is something they never *volunteer* to do.

"Sorry." I apologize for their rudeness. I've been doing that a lot lately…to principals, teachers and now uncles.

"It's hard for them," he says, as understanding as ever. "I should have known better than to mention the barbecue."

I wave a hand. "I'm glad you brought it up. There's something I'd forgotten I was supposed to do."

He catches my hand and the card grasped in it. "What's this?"

"Your inheritance. Rob bequeathed this to you some time ago."

I just wish he'd done the same with the lamp. I am beginning to feel guilty about keeping her locked away in the closet. If only I knew someone who would enjoy the tacky thing.

That someone is not Keith. Even his casual wear, of buttoned-down oxford and khakis, is classy. What is Pam thinking to throw away a catch this good? I shake my head, unable to comprehend the workings of my oldest sister's muddled mind.

Keith is smiling as he reads the card. It's good to see him like this. "Brown sugar." He chuckles.

"Figures, doesn't it?"

He nods as he slips the card into his shirt pocket, then pats it. "When they're ready—" he gestures toward the hall with the closed bedroom doors "—I'll barbe-cue."

I appreciate that he understands and is willing to wait for them to come around. But then I guess he has practice as he waits for Pam to do the same. Hopefully her cruise has brought her more clarity than Rob's death.

"You'll barbecue," I agree, "but you don't have to use Rob's recipe. Just between us, I always liked yours better." It wasn't so sweet; it had a bite to it.

Keith grins. "You're lucky Rob can't hear you." His face falls. "I'm sorry—that was horribly insensitive."

He thinks that was insensitive? I should tell him what I got Claire for her birthday, but I don't want to think about how much I hurt her. Using Mom's patented gesture of reassurance, I squeeze his hand. "Don't worry."

I hope Rob *can* hear me, otherwise I've wasted an awful lot of time cursing him to myself.

"Hey, where's that bottle of wine I brought?" Keith asks, probably eager to change the uncomfortable subject.

At least he tries. I have so many friends who, fearing the uncomfortable, don't make the offer to talk to me at all. That's okay, though. I don't need friends when I have family. I often try to point that out to Claire, who is still swearing that she doesn't need anyone. I hope she will befriend her stepcousin the way Robbie has. In fact, I would prefer that Robbie didn't and just Claire did. Melissa is nothing like her punked-out brother. She's a sweet girl, probably too sweet-natured to deal with Claire's waspish tongue, though.

I sigh, suddenly eager for the wine. I bring it out of the fridge where I had it chilling. Keith makes a face. I guess it's one of those you're supposed to drink warm.

"Sorry." But I'm not. The thought of drinking warm wine makes my tongue dry, unless it's sweet like Lambrusco. Unfortunately, that doesn't appeal to me anymore, either.

"It's okay," he says, but he makes another face as I hand him the cheap plastic-handled corkscrew.

I'm tempted to make a faux pas trifecta and bring out plastic wineglasses, but I reach for the crystal ones instead. These were a gift from him and Pam. As he pours the pale liquid into the glasses, light shines through the crystal, creating prisms of color. Mini-rainbows in a glass.

"Beautiful," he says.

I glance to where the sun is setting off the deck. "Yes. Let's go outside."

He opens the patio door and slides it closed behind me. We stand quietly at the railing for a while, watching the sun set in an explosion of red, orange and pink. No expensive man-made fireworks can recreate such intense color.

Rob tried. For years he'd gone to Indiana, breaking the law to bring home the most expensive and most illegal of fireworks. I see the hole in the woods behind the house where he caught them on fire a couple years ago, leaving a bare patch of ground where once pine and oaks had stood. Life with Rob had been one adventure after another, some more fun than others.

"Do you like the wine?" Keith asks, reminding me that I haven't taken a sip.

I try it, finding it tart and crisp. "This is good." Something that would suit salad; I should have served it with dinner. We'd had strawberry-and-walnut salad with lime-pepper chicken breasts.

"I'm glad you like it."

I'm glad we have this minute alone.

"Keith, I appreciate you making an effort with the kids." And letting me use you for their male influence.

He nods. "I care about them. I can't imagine how difficult this is for them. And you."

"In a way, I think you can," I say.

He sighs. "I'm alone now." He takes another sip, then turns toward me. "How do you handle being alone, Holly?"

"I'm not. I have my kids."

Even though they fight me, I'm not giving up on them. Our trip to the mall a few days ago went well, which was a pleasant surprise after the fiasco that was Claire's birthday party.

He reveals that he's not unaware of the tension in our house when he says, "You're alone."

I take another sip of the wine.

"I don't want to be alone, Holly."

I hear the pain and vulnerability in his voice. I set my wineglass down to take his hand. I can't offer him any "you'll be fine" platitudes. I hated when people offered those to me, so I just squeeze his hand.

He dips his head.

I close my eyes, expecting an appreciative kiss on the

cheek, but his lips are on mine, moving, with appreciation not for my sympathy but my gender. He's not kissing me as a brother, he's kissing me as a man kisses a woman.

I jerk away, tripping over a lawn chair as I step back. "Keith!"

"Oh, God, Holly…" He's as appalled by what he did as I am. "I'm sorry. You know that Rob was my best friend. I would never…"

But Rob's dead and Pam's gone, and he's lonely, lonely in a way that I've never been nor will ever be. Keith needs to be with someone, anyone.

I just need to be with Rob.

"I know, Keith. It's okay. We'll blame it on the wine." Even though we both barely had a glass. "And the sunset."

He nods, his face as red as the sun, which has left the sky. "I better go home…."

I don't want him to leave like this, awkwardly, embarrassed, but I don't want him to stay, either.

"I'll hold you to that barbecue," I say as I see him to the front door.

He pats his shirt pocket where Rob's recipe is tucked. Then he salutes me and starts down the driveway to his house.

Oh, Keith…

When I was thirteen, I dreamed of his kisses. Now I'll probably have nightmares, not just of Keith's kiss but any man's but Rob's.

How am I supposed to deal with giving up that part of my life—kisses, passion? Am I supposed to join a convent?

Again the laughter echoes inside my head. Rob's. At least one of us is amused. I'm not finding any humor at the thought of myself in a habit and support hose. But that's a far better option than the alternative.

Dating.

STAGE 9

I should have let Deputy Westmoreland talk to me at The Tearoom the other day instead of rushing off like I did. Now I've spent the last few days wondering *what* exactly he needed to talk to me about.

Possibilities have my stomach churning. I'd rather blame my indigestion on the deputy and not what happened after dinner with Keith. My stomach could be upset because of my chicken, but it wasn't undercooked. And it wasn't the wine, since it was too good. No, I'm blaming the deputy.

So I'm at the counter in the kitchen, sipping a glass of ginger ale, when I see headlights from a car pulling into the driveway. It's late for a school night—eleven. The kids have been in bed almost an hour already.

Pam must be back. She had such crazy flight times, both there and back, that she drove herself to the airport in Grand Rapids and parked her car in the long-term lot. It's good that she'd come here straight from the airport, since it must mean she's figured something out. Of course, if she figured out what I hope she has, she would be pulling into her and Keith's driveway, not mine.

I set down my glass and walk toward the front door. Ordinarily I'd open up the garage for her, but I suspect she's not staying. I'm anxious to hear what she has to say, but when I turn on the porch light and see what's actually parked in the driveway, I'm anxious about something else entirely. It isn't Pam's champagne-colored Volvo station wagon, but a police car. A navy-blue one with a gold emblem on the door, a county car. I know before he even steps out that it's Deputy Westmoreland.

Obviously he *really* needs to talk to me. What about?

Did Smiley finally decide to press charges? Maybe that was the reason for the intense exchange between him and my mother the same day that the deputy told me we needed to talk.

Is Deputy Westmoreland here to arrest me for vandalizing Smiley's store? But is destroying Kitty Cupcakes a crime punishable by the police department or animal control or maybe the food inspector?

I suppress a nervous giggle. I don't really believe his visit has anything to do with that incident. It was too long ago. My thoughts are confirmed when he opens the back door of his police cruiser and helps my son out.

Heedless of my flannel pajamas, I run out to the car. "Robbie!"

He won't look at me. But even with his head down,

some of the porch light glistens on the tear tracks drying on his face. My heart contracts, and I gasp for a breath.

"He's not hurt," Westmoreland says, somehow reading my mind.

Not yet. But he might be. "Robbie, you're supposed to be in bed."

He obviously snuck out, and I didn't catch him. The deputy did.

"What did he do?" I ask, as Robbie's not talking.

"Shoplifting in Smiley's store."

Because of the party aisle, Smiley's is open late, but Robbie shouldn't have been there doing anything. He should have been in his bed, where I thought he was.

"Shoplifting?" I say it breathlessly, as if someone has sucker-punched me, which I think he has. Deputy Westmoreland. Not Robbie. It's the second time he's made me feel this way. I don't like it. Or him.

I know Robbie is the one I should be angry with, but he's just standing there, silently crying next to the police car in which he's ridden home.

Even though Robbie's not denying it, I do. "He would never do something like that."

Not the son I knew. But I remind myself that lately, I've been living with strangers.

"He did," the deputy maintains. "I caught him doing it myself."

Red-handed. And red-faced. In the porch light, Robbie's face flushes bright crimson.

"But you didn't arrest him?" I ask.

"Smiley didn't want to press charges this time."

"There won't be a next." Seeing Robbie's tears makes me want to cry, too. "What did he take?"

I'm so hoping he wasn't in that party aisle. There is no cupcake display there anymore, just alcohol.

"Cigarettes."

I laugh, a quick reflex of relief. "He has asthma. There's no way he intended to smoke."

"Mom!" This is Robbie's first comment, a protest of my release of his medical information. I think the alert bracelet on his wrist might have given as much away as I have.

"Robbie." I want to say more. I want to scream and yell at him. It's not the deputy's watchful presence stopping me. It's myself. Robbie is more lost to me now than the night he ran away.

"I know he wasn't taking the cigarettes for himself," the deputy interjects into our awkward silence. "He won't tell me who put him up to it."

I know, and so does the deputy. I catch his furtive glance toward Emma's house. The floodlight on the barn illuminates her entire yard and the car sitting in her drive, mud camouflaging the red paint. Troy may not let Emma tell him how to raise his kids, but tomorrow I will. Maybe tonight, once I get rid of the deputy.

"Robbie," I say again.

He still won't look at me, probably afraid I'm going to yell, like I want to, or grill him, like the deputy probably already has. Are those tears he's silently shedding in fear of my reaction or because of what the deputy has already said to him? I need to know.

But *he's* not the one who's going to tell me.

"Robbie, go to bed. You have school in the morning." A little shoplifting isn't going to get him out of that.

He won't look at me, but he glances up at the deputy, silently asking his permission when he has no problem sneaking out without mine. The deputy nods, and then and only then does my son do what I've told him. He skedaddles into the house, sending one last, fearful glance over his shoulder before closing the front door.

"What did you do to him?" I ask, the words vibrating in the air between us. I'm shaking with anger and nerves and fear. I am more scared than Robbie is.

"What?" The deputy takes a step back, probably worrying that I'm going to attack him again.

"He's a minor. You're not supposed to question a minor without a parent present." I only think this because of what I've heard on *Law & Order*, but it makes sense.

The deputy nods. "I could have called you to come down to Smiley's."

But I know why he didn't. He wanted to save me the embarrassment, because of what I did in the store not that long ago. I should be grateful.

Instead, I'm even madder. "You should have!"

"Or I could have taken him to the police department and called you down there," he points out, his voice all gravelly with irritation.

"You said Smiley didn't press charges." This time. I remember exactly what he said.

"No, he didn't. If this were any other town, charges would be pressed."

I don't think he's talking just about Robbie's shoplifting stunt now. I ball my hand into a fist, thinking about hitting him again, when he regretfully shakes his head. "I'm sorry, Mrs. DeJong."

Earlier I'd told him to call me Holly. I'm glad he doesn't now. My driveway in the dark hardly seems the place for a first-name basis.

"So am I," I confess. About so many things. "I appreciate your bringing Robbie home."

I move to step around him, to follow my son into the house, but Westmoreland puts a hand on my arm, his fingers closing over the flannel sleeve. Sheep squirm beneath his grasp.

"I want to do more than that," he says.

I must be just noticing the cool autumn air now, for I shiver. "Wh—at?" Since my voice cracks, I try again. "What do you want to do?"

"This is what I wanted to talk to you about the other day."

Before I ran away from him. I want to run again, but he's holding on to me. That must be why.

"I want to work with Robbie."

As one of his at-risk teens. My shy, computer geek son, at risk? Then I remember what I need to add to that description because of tonight. My shy, computer geek, sneaking-out-of-the-house, shoplifting-cigarettes son.

I need to accept what he has become.

It would be easy to turn him over to the officer, to make him someone else's responsibility. But I can't do that.

Even though he's become a stranger, he's mine.

So I won't ship him off to military school, but I might make our home into one, with bars on the windows and barbed wire fencing around the yard. No one will be sneaking out again, even if I have to give up sleeping to guard the door.

My hands are shaking so badly when I reach for the lamp that I knock the box off the shelf in the walk-in closet. It bounces off the rod of clothes and clatters to the floor. That was an accident, but I feel this dizzying flash of vindication. So I pick up the box and hurl it out of the closet. End over end, it rolls across the carpet like a stone skipping across water. But my gesture isn't carefree.

Nothing about my life has been since Rob died. I walk the few paces to where the box has stopped, lying on its side. I lift my foot, aim the toe of my slipper and kick the cardboard. Now dented, the box rolls again, drunkenly, to within a couple feet of the door.

The vindication is gone. Like stomping on Kitty Cupcakes, beating up the hula lamp solves none of my problems. All I feel now is remorse. I drop to my knees beside the box, and worried that I've broken it, peel back the flaps, my heart in my throat.

Except for a dented shade, she's fine. The package of Kitty Cupcakes cushioned her. I guess it's not a bad thing I forgot they were in the bottom of the box. Maybe they're actually good for something.

I never could understand what Rob saw in them, but then I've never eaten one. The cellophane window, below where the kitty is licking her whiskers, is broken. Maybe the toe of my slipper broke it; maybe a coconut boob smashed it out. I'll never know. But for some reason I can't stop staring at the box. Tonight—or is it morning now?—Kitty Cupcakes fascinate me more than the lamp.

I've had a rough night. If I need a crutch to get through what's left of it, I could reach for the bottle of wine I have left in the fridge. I don't *need* chocolate. But right now I'm weak.

Leaving the box sealed, I reach through the broken window and pull out an individually wrapped cupcake. I shouldn't be tempted. My stomach is upset, and even if it wasn't, it's full of good food, a delicately seasoned chicken breast, strawberry, walnuts and greens drizzled with light poppy-seed dressing—none of that is junk.

This is.

My hand closes tightly around the wrapper. I should crush it the way I crushed that whole display in Smiley's. Instead I pop it open, the package sighing as if in ecstasy, as I release the cake into my hand. Frosting oozes between my fingers.

I have to know. I have to know why Rob couldn't stop eating these things even after those few first heart attacks. Surely he felt the pain of those, but he risked another. For these. Knowing Rob, he didn't think it was serious; nothing ever was with him. He probably wrote it off as a bad case of heartburn. But still he wouldn't give up what caused it. He never gave up.

My hand is shaking as I lift the cupcake toward my mouth. I bite it like I'm biting a tag off a new outfit when I'm too impatient to look for scissors. My teeth are brutal, tearing, then my lips close around the cake. The frosting oozes across my tongue now, melting.

My taste buds sigh like the paper did…in ecstasy.

The cake is sweet and moist. The frosting is dark and bitter. The filling is creamy and sweet. The combination is euphoric. And now I understand Rob.

How do I understand Robbie?

Do I smoke a pack of cigarettes? Do I make him smoke one until he turns blue and I have to take him to the hospital? That's what would happen if he tried one. He knows that.

And he knows better than to steal.

I need to talk to him. But when I came in the house from turning down the deputy's offer of help, Robbie's light was off. He was tucked into his bed already, pretending to be asleep. I could have woken him.

But it wouldn't help either of us to talk when I'm this upset, upset enough to cross over to the dark side. I reach for a twin to the cupcake I've just devoured. As I gobble it down, I tweak the lamp so the girl starts swaying.

Is this how Rob would have handled parenting issues if he'd been the one to survive me? Stupid question. It was how he'd handled everything. Food and humor.

But maybe he was onto something. Because, ironically, the chocolate settles my stomach, the swaying doll my nerves. I'll be better able to deal with Robbie in the morning, after I've gotten some sleep. And he'll have all night to worry about *how* I'm going to deal with him.

* * *

"Why do we have to do this?" Robbie whines from the passenger's seat.

"You know why. Smiley was nice enough to not press charges against you, or you would have spent the night in jail. You owe him an apology and a thank-you."

"You would have bailed me out," Robbie says, pushing up his glasses.

"Would I? It might have done you good to spend the night with Bubba and Guido."

He snorts. "There's nobody named Bubba or Guido in Stanville."

"You don't know that. They might have been passing through and decided to break the law last night. Seems a lot of people were acting crazy last night."

Like me.

I woke up with chocolate smeared across my cheek and my pillow. I feel like I woke up with a stranger after a drunken, one-night stand. But *I* am that stranger. I avoid the rearview mirror just as Robbie avoids meeting my eyes.

"Yeah." He miraculously agrees with me. "A lot of people were."

This morning isn't a whole lot better.

Claire isn't happy about being excluded from whatever is going on between her brother and me—I didn't tell her about last night. I simply dropped her at

Emma's, knowing her aunt will make her get on the bus. I didn't tell Emma anything, either. Yet. But later we will have a talk about Jason. I missed Troy this morning; he'd already left for work.

I might stop down there after I drop Robbie at school, but first he and I have another stop to make. It's too early for Smiley to be at the store, so we pull into the condo complex where he lives. His unit is just a couple over from my mom. I'm hoping she doesn't see the car, though, since I really don't want to tell her what her grandson did last night. My mother's pride is smarting too much. I taught my children *not* to steal. How could he forget that?

Rob and I didn't have many rules, but that was a biggie. Bigger than the no-swearing one. We would have doled out a severe punishment for breaking it. I fully intend to; this is just phase one.

I park the Tahoe in front of Smiley's one-stall garage and open my door. Robbie doesn't even reach for his.

"I don't understand why I have to do this," he whines again. I suspect he didn't get much sleep last night, either.

"Did *you* apologize after you smashed up his store?" he asks me.

"I didn't smash up the store. I fell over one display." I'd like to make it sound like an accident, but I know that ship has sailed. "Okay, I *lost* it."

"So did I," he says, and his changing voice has finally decided on a tone. Deep.

"Why, Robbie?"

My hope lifts; this could be it. The breakthrough when he'll start confiding in me again and I'll get to know this stranger.

Instead he throws open the door. "Let's do this."

"Let's," I concur. I will apologize, too. It's long overdue, and it'll probably save Mom from any more intense conversations with the store owner.

We follow the short cement walk to Smiley's door, where I press the bell. We wait for a few minutes before hearing fumbling at the door, and it's pulled open. Smiley stands there, his white brows lifted high, his dark eyes not so sharp this morning. His hair is standing up, too, and he wears a flannel robe so loosely tied that white tufts of chest hair peek out from between the lapels.

"I should have called first." I say it as I think it. "I'm sorry to bother you so early—"

"It must be important," Smiley says, stepping back to usher us inside. "Or you wouldn't have tracked her down here."

Her?

"We came to see—"

My mother walking out of Smiley's bedroom, if his floor plan is the same as hers. She has only one bedroom on the main floor, a guest suite finished in the basement, and the one-stall garage. She swore it was all she needed after Dad died. That's why she sold the farm and the house where we all grew up. She didn't need all that room anymore.

She's wearing only a robe, too. It's hard to say who's more surprised, her or me, as she exclaims, "Holly! Robbie!"

"I'm sorry," I say.

This isn't part of the planned apology to Smiley. This is a knee-jerk reaction to seeing something I didn't want to see and am sorry that I have. I back out the door, pulling Robbie with me.

"Holly," my mother says again. She's calmer now but no less horrified than I am.

"We'll talk later," I tell her, but I wonder if I'm not lying to her like I lied to Claire on her birthday. Right now, I just want to get out of here.

"I'm sorry," Robbie says to Smiley. "About what I did last night."

I should be proud that he stuck to the purpose of our visit when I'm horribly sidetracked. Once I'm back behind the wheel of the Tahoe, I'm too confused to put the key in the ignition and start the engine.

Robbie leans back in his seat with a sigh. "Now you know how I felt last night…when I saw you and Uncle Keith kissing. At least Grandpa's been dead a long time. Dad hasn't."

And now I know why *he* snapped.

STAGE 10

"Y̲ou could have given me a day to rest before throwing me back into work at The Tearoom," Pam complains this afternoon as she settles into a patio chair on the back deck where her husband kissed me just the night before.

And my son saw and went on a crime spree. Well, as big a crime spree as one can have in Stanville.

"I had a situation with Robbie," I explain truthfully. It's probably all I'll share with her. I'm still trying to figure out fact from fiction myself.

"Do you want to talk about it?" she asks.

I shake my head. "No. Let's talk about your cruise. Tell me all about the Bahamas."

"Should we wait for Emma?"

After the conversation I had with Troy this afternoon, I don't think so. He might ban her from my house the way he banned her from his kids' rooms. "No."

She swirls the wine in her glass, studying it. Then

she sniffs it, analyzing all those things people like Rob and me, with our screw-top Lambrusco, are blissfully unaware of. "You've had Keith over," she says.

"Yes." I brace myself for another of her tantrums.

She only lifts an eyebrow, surprisingly calm. "Want to talk about that?"

No. "I was worried about him. Let's talk about your cruise."

"We should really wait for Emma—"

"You won't mind repeating it." I know her too well.

She laughs. "Yes, I won't." She stretches in the chair almost as if she's about to purr like the kitten Claire wouldn't accept. "It was wonderful."

She doesn't have to tell me that. I can see from her tan and her smiling face that she's happier and more relaxed than I've ever seen her. She's barely reacted to Keith being over here, not at all like her reaction when he'd helped search for Robbie. But she doesn't know about the kiss.

Maybe I should tell her.

Robbie might. Even though I explained to him that I was no part of that kiss and it was just a mistake on Keith's part, I'm not sure he believes me. If he really wants to get back at me, telling Pam would be much more effective than stealing cigarettes from Smiley's.

"I'm so relaxed." She rubs it in. "So happy."

"Who is he?" I ask.

She chokes on a sip of wine. "W-what?" she stammers after catching her breath.

"Who's the guy you left Keith for?"

Because I know the truth about Mom, and that she wasn't just busy baking for The Tearoom or with condo stuff all those times she was unavailable for us, things are starting to add up about Pam. "All the classes and shopping in Grand Rapids. This trip all by yourself."

Pam jumps to her feet, either insulted or feeling guilty as hell that I've caught her. Mom might have been sneaking around, but at least what she's done isn't adultery.

Although somehow it feels that way.

All I've been able to think about today is my dad. I haven't thought about him much lately, so it's odd, but I know why. Even though he's been gone years, I feel as if Mom betrayed him, like Robbie feels I betrayed his father.

"I shouldn't have to explain myself to *you*," Pam says, greatly affronted. "You're my sister. You know me better than that, and you should trust me."

I trust no one right now. Not my lying mother nor my thieving son.

"What's his name?" I insist.

Pam lifts her hand, and I think she's about to slap me. But instead she turns to the railing and curls her fingers around it. I wait for it. The confession.

"There is someone else," she admits.

I suspected it, but having it confirmed makes me sick all over again. "Pam…"

"Me." She swings back toward me, her eyes hard with anger. "I shop in Grand Rapids because there's nothing in Stanville I like. Smiley's taste and mine aren't exactly the same."

If she only knew…

"And I take my classes there for the same reason. Mrs. Diller doesn't teach what I'm interested in."

For a minute I've forgotten that's where Claire is, taking extra lessons with Mrs. Diller. It's the one interest she's retained from her previous life, probably because Rob loved so much to hear her play.

"And I took the trip alone because I wanted to be alone," she says slowly and succinctly. "That's why I'm getting divorced. I went straight from living with Mom and Dad and you and Emma to living with Keith, and shortly after, Rachael. I want to live *alone* now."

I get it. I've had glimmers of understanding before, but this is when it truly sinks in. Pam wants to be alone. Keith can't stand being alone. Maybe they never really had anything in common.

"I'm sorry," I say.

"You should be." She sighs. "You know the greatest part of my trip?"

I shake my head and wish I was really interested, but

I'm not. Pam has her life figured out, and I'm happy for her, truly I am, but I'm also worried about her collateral damage.

"Not having to talk to anyone. I just lay in the sun on deck, reading and thinking. It was heaven."

Her definition is different from mine. The only thing we have in common is being sisters.

Someone knocks on the patio door before pulling it open. "There you are," Mom says as she joins us.

Pam glances back and forth between us, for once not oblivious to the tension. "This isn't some kind of intervention, is it? Where you're both going to try to talk me into going back to Keith?"

So Pam knows Mom knows about her filing. Had she finally confessed? From her defensive attitude, I assume Mom wasn't as understanding as she hoped.

Mom shakes her head. "I want to talk to Holly. Alone." But she doesn't look at me.

"So what, you can pump her for information about me? Is that why you asked me about someone else?" Pam demands. She's more than offended now; she's mad.

It wouldn't be the first time Mom has pumped me for information about her or Emma, so the conclusions she's jumped to are as logical as Pam ever is.

"No," Mom says. "Not everything is about you, Pam. I'll see you in the morning."

Pam hasn't fought with Mom since she was a teenager. I think she's considering it, but then she puts down her wineglass and walks away.

"I really can't talk now," I say to Mom. "I have to pick Claire up from Mrs. Diller's."

"Holly, don't treat me like your children are treating you," she says. "Don't shut me out. You're an adult. You need to tell me how you're feeling, so we can deal with it."

I need a damn cupcake right now. But in lieu of chocolate, I'll take time. "We'll have to deal later," I insist, forcing a regretful smile, even though I truly feel none in postponing this discussion. "I have to pick up Claire."

And I need time to overcome my initial shock and to accept that my mother is a woman, too. Like I used to be, back when I shared my bed with my husband. I'm not sure what I am now.

I'm late.

Claire's sitting on the step that leads down to the sidewalk just outside Mrs. Diller's picket fence. She's rocking back and forth. Amusing herself because I'm late?

She doesn't stand up when I stop next to her. I figure it's because she's mad—she has a right to be. No one likes to be forgotten. It's not her fault I had other stuff going on today.

I shut off the Tahoe and open the door. "Claire…"

She looks up and I see the tears streaming down her face. She wouldn't get that upset over my being late. "Honey, what's the matter?"

"She's dead."

That's when I notice Bill Diller's car in his mother's driveway. Next to that is a navy-blue county police car.

"Oh, my God, what happened?" I drag her up and into my arms.

Instead of pulling away, she clings. "Mom, she just…she just…" She gasps for breath on a hiccupping sob. "Died."

"Oh, honey."

"I was playing and looked over. I thought she fell asleep…."

I hug her tighter and rub soothing circles on her shaking back.

"But I couldn't wake her up. So I called Mr. Diller."

Mr. Diller. Not me. Something shifts in my chest, hurting. I wish she had called me.

"He called 911, but it was too late…." She dissolves into wrenching sobs.

I don't remember her crying this hard for her father, not that I begrudge Mrs. Diller any tears. She was a sweet woman. In fact, a few tears trail down my face. "It's okay, Claire."

"No, no, it's not!" she shrieks. "Everyone I care about dies!"

Again something tightens in my chest. Maybe it's Kitty's revenge. One package of cupcakes and I'm having a heart attack already. I help Claire into the passenger's side of the Tahoe, then push her hair back from her face.

"I'm here, Claire," I tell her. "I'll always be here for you and your brother."

It's a big promise to make, especially as I can't really control keeping it. I'll toss out the rest of the cupcakes when I get home, but what about lightning? You never know when that'll strike. It can actually be a sunny day....

I close her door and walk around the back to the driver's side, but I don't make it all the way there. The deputy is standing by the rear bumper.

"Is she all right?"

"No thanks to you." I rip into him. "You didn't call me again! What, were you just going to drive her home, too?"

And give me a heart attack for real when he took my second child out of his back seat.

"I called," he says. "Your mother answered. She gave me your cell number, which I called."

"But I—"

His tone is full of exasperation when he adds, "She answered that, too."

I left my phone on the charger. But somehow that

must be *his* fault. Everything is. I move to shove past him, but he grabs my shoulder. First my hand the other day, now he's moving up. Will his next grab be my hair?

But the image that flashes through my mind isn't of him dragging me off to a cave somewhere. The surface I imagine is much softer than that, his hand in my hair for another reason entirely. I shut my eyes tightly, suppressing the traitorous image.

"I don't have time to deal with you," I tell him.

"I know you have your hands full, and I want to help." His voice vibrates with frustration and irritation.

Like mine. "I don't need *your* help."

"Holly—"

This time I manage to pull away. "I have to get my daughter home." Behind the bars and barbed wire—not to keep her in like Robbie, but to keep her safe from any more pain. I'm determined she never gets hurt again.

Mom stayed. She's sitting on the deck, in the dark. I know this, not because I've joined her but because her car is still in the driveway and she left dinner on the counter for us. Robbie ate with her earlier. Claire won't eat at all. She's lying down in my bed right now, exhausted from the day's events.

I'm exhausted, too. I don't have anything left for the

discussion my mother must still want to have. But I open the patio door and step onto the deck, into the cool night air and the dark.

"Poor Bill," she says, her voice shaky. "He and his mother were so close."

Is she trying to tell me something? She and I have always been close, or so I thought. But I didn't know then that she was keeping secrets from me.

"Poor Claire," I say, with a weary sigh.

"You couldn't get her to eat." She confirms that she was watching us through the glass…and listening.

I bristle, taking her comment as criticism of my parenting, something she's never done. Until recently, I was a good parent. I didn't forget to pick up my daughter from her piano teacher. I didn't have a son shoplifting from his grandmother's lover's store.

"I can't do this anymore," I say, letting her take it how she wants. Our conversation. Or parenting. I'm beginning to worry I can't do that alone. Maybe I was only a good parent with Rob.

"I'm sorry," she says, and doesn't add any clarification either. Is she sorry about her criticism or keeping her relationship with Smiley secret?

I'm too emotionally wrung out to care. Claire's tears drained me. I lean against the railing and stare at the dark woods.

"I can't be like you," my mother adds.

"How's that?" I ask, confused. Maybe she's making sense, but I'm too tired to comprehend.

"I know you think I'm strong, but I'm not."

And I am?

"I couldn't stay here on the farm after your father died. That's why I moved. It had nothing to do with starting something for myself. It was that I wasn't strong enough to handle the pain of being here…without your father."

"I understand that." I'd thought about selling the house, too. More than once. Moving away from my dream house that's a nightmare to live in alone. Moving to another city to start a business that will keep me as happy and vital as The Tearoom keeps my mother. But with the kids' reaction to the sale of the business, I don't dare. And now I realize that it probably isn't The Tearoom that has made my mother happy, but Smiley.

"I can't even think about your father now, six years later, without it hurting," she continues. "And it still bothers me to come out here, to remember how much he loved being here…."

I hear the catch of grief in her voice and go to her now, dropping to my knees at her feet. "Oh, Mom…"

"I haven't replaced your father," she says, "if that's what you think."

I'd like to say I am more upset about the lying. But

I can't, although I do wonder how they kept their relationship secret in *this* town. "That's not fair to you, Mom, for me to think that. It's been six years."

I can't expect her to live alone. She's a vibrant woman who's entitled to male companionship, to happiness. But with someone other than my father? It shouldn't bother me anymore, but since it does, it raises another question for me. How will my kids ever deal with my getting involved with someone else?

My mother sighs so hard my hair stirs from her breath. "This…thing with Smiley…"

I'm amused that she doesn't even know what to call it.

"It didn't just start," she admits.

That tightness constricts my chest again. But still I ask, "When?"

"Almost six years ago."

"But Dad…"

"It was *after* he died."

She's going on about Smiley understanding because he lost the love of his life, too—his wife—just a couple years before my father died. Just as she'd poured herself into The Tearoom, he'd become obsessed with the store. There's more, but I can hardly hear what she's saying.

It's a morbid question to ask, but for some reason I have to know. "How long after?"

"Three weeks."

The pain in my chest threatens to burst. I stand up and step back from her.

"That's why I couldn't tell you and your sisters. You were already mad at me for selling the farm."

That wasn't all she sold out. It's not that I expect her to still be mourning him. Okay, maybe I do. But three weeks?

"So that's why you didn't tell us then. But it's been six years. Why would you keep it from us for so long?" It's ridiculous, something over which Rob would have laughed heartily—senior citizens carrying on a secret affair.

She shrugs, and even in the dim light on the deck, I can see her face redden. "Smiley tried convincing me to make our relationship public. But I didn't want the town talking about us, speculating about us."

"I don't know how you kept it secret so long."

She shrugs again. "It wasn't easy."

"What about us? Why couldn't you tell us?" I ask.

"It hurt so much to lose your father. I couldn't risk losing you or your sisters. You've all already been upset with me for selling the farm."

"And that was wrong," I admit, feeling petty and selfish for having ever doubted the way Mom had grieved. Then or now.

"And I was wrong not to tell you all the truth. I realized that this morning. The look on your face…" Instead of crying, she starts giggling. "It really was priceless."

"I'm glad *you* can find the humor," I say. She and Rob were so much alike. Would he have moved on with someone else that quickly? With a sinking sensation, I realize that he probably would have. Like Keith, he hadn't liked to be alone. He needed an appreciative audience.

"You always could, Holly," Mom says.

"I guess I lost my sense of humor," I reply.

"You don't lose something like that. It's a part of you. It's what enabled you to see what a great guy Rob was, and take a chance on him."

I had taken some convincing to even go out with him. When I first met him at the coffee shop where I'd worked on campus, I thought he was loud and obnoxious with his silly jokes and booming laugh.

I wasn't wrong.

But what I missed at the first meeting, and learned all the subsequent times he came in to ask me out, was that he was also very sweet and generous. Although my opinion of his generosity was tempered by the fact that he kept ripping my five-dollar tips in half, refusing to give me the other half until I gave him my phone number. Eventually I did, and from the first date, we were inseparable.

"You're going to need that sense of humor," Mom cautions me. "Raising teenagers is tough enough with someone helping you. But by yourself…"

"I'll be fine, Mom," I assure her. "The kids will be fine, too." Now I'm the one lying. Like mother, like daughter.

In the darkness, I see her smile as a glint of white teeth. She knows, but doesn't call me on my lie. She puts me on the spot about something else entirely. "Will *we* be okay?"

I nod. She's my mother, and I love her. But I don't understand her nearly as well as I thought I did. "Sure we will."

"Good, because I still want you to work at The Tearoom with me."

Now my stomach tightens into knots. "Mom, of course I'll keep doing the books, but Pam's back."

"We both know you're better with customers than Pam is. Everybody loves you. And although you may not believe you and I are very much alike anymore, I think you need the place as much as I do."

Inadvertently she's confirmed my suspicion that if I asked, she'd sell me the business. She's also confirmed that it still means too much to her for her to be happy about selling.

She continues, "It gives a balance to your life. You need that balance now, Holly. As much as you want to focus on your kids, it's not going to be healthy for any of you if that's all you have in your life." She reaches for my hand and squeezes it tight. "You need *more*, Holly."

I hope she's still talking about just the restaurant. I can't follow anything else from her widow guidebook. Even with Rob gone over seven months, it would be too soon for me to get involved with anyone else. Forever may be too soon. I can suppress my needs without exploding; I'm pretty sure I can...

STAGE 11

I didn't get much sleep due to sharing my bed with Claire. I hadn't had the heart to wake her and have her sleep in her own bed. Having her next to me, whimpering in her sleep, reminded me of the times she'd crawled into our bed when she was a little girl, scared from a nightmare. But now she's bigger than I am and sleeps restlessly, swinging her arms and kicking her legs, so that I slept on the edge of the mattress. My back is aching, and I'm sure to be sporting bruises.

I left her sleeping this morning and had to explain to Robbie why it's okay for her to skip school today and for him *not* to. He'd barely known Mrs. Diller. And Claire…I'd had no idea how attached she was to the older woman. She'd been taking lessons from the retired music teacher since she was only six or seven, though.

I called the grief counselor after Robbie caught the bus, and told her what had happened and Claire's reaction. She believes Claire is not just grieving her piano teacher's death but the loss of her father all over again.

My heart hurts for her, but I can't mourn Rob again. Like my mother, who had to sell the farm to avoid memories of my father, it just hurts *too much*.

Like my back. I'm wrestling with the childproof cap on a bottle of aspirin when the front door opens. "Robbie, if you missed that bus—"

"He got on the bus. I waited," Emma says. Her eyes are red-rimmed, and her face is tight. I don't think she got much more sleep than I did. Did she know Mrs. Diller as well as Claire? Or is it just her soft heart commiserating?

"Where's Claire?" she asks.

"Sleeping." At least one of us will have more than a couple hours, no matter how restlessly she's "resting."

"Then I won't scream and yell," Emma says. "I'll just quietly tell you how pissed off I am at you."

And like any parent knows, sometimes that quiet tone is more effective than yelling. "Okay…"

"You had no right to go to Troy."

Oh. *That*.

With everything else that had happened in the past twenty-four-plus hours, I'd forgotten about doing that. In retrospect, I probably shouldn't have gone to Troy's garage after dropping off Robbie at school, after discovering my mother's secret relationship with Smiley.

"I can't believe you would go to his place of work,"

Emma says, her whisper waspish, "and talk to him that way...."

I could do some damage control by explaining the situation and my frame of mind, but as she'd left last night, my mother had begged me to promise I wouldn't tell Pam or Emma about her *thing* with Smiley until she had the chance.

But Troy had become the cupcake over more than my mother's secret love life. I honestly believe the biggest reason my son has become a stranger to me has been due to his stepcousin's influence.

"Emma, do you really believe Robbie was stealing those cigarettes for himself?"

Her face flushes with a little more red than from her temper. "No, but you have no proof that Jason had anything to do with it. Deputy Westmoreland didn't catch *him* stealing."

"No. *He* was too smart to get caught." Robbie is not, which is a good thing. I do not want my son to be good at crime. "But you and I both know he was there. Robbie didn't get from here to town on his own steam. He would have passed out before he got there."

Especially if he'd smoked one of the cigarettes.

Emma's head lowers; she can't look at me anymore. "I'm sorry, Holly."

I've been getting a lot of ambiguous apologies lately. Is she sorry my son has asthma or for yelling at me?

"I actually asked Jason to reach out to Robbie after Rob died," she explains. "Since his mother abandoned him, I thought he would be able to identify with Robbie."

"Rob did *not* abandon him."

Sure, he should have quit eating his contraband sweets, but Rob was never a quitter. Yes, he should have paid attention to the warning chest pains and gone to a doctor, but he probably hadn't taken them seriously, as he'd taken so little. He wouldn't have chosen to leave his family; he'd loved us all too much. I will have to remind myself of that the next time *I* feel as if he's abandoned us. Because I have felt that way, especially when I'm dealing with being a single parent.

"Do you think Robbie knows that?" Emma asks.

Maybe in his heart; in his head, I'm not too sure. He hasn't been making the greatest decisions lately. I shrug. "I don't know."

"The kid needs someone to talk to," Emma insists.

"I don't want Jason to be that someone." *I* want to be that someone.

"You should have told *me* that, not Troy."

"Why?" I ask, getting mad now myself, but for Emma, not Robbie. "You can't tell his children what to do or not to do. He won't let you."

"They're his kids." Emma defends him, faintly.

"You're raising those kids, too. They're as much

yours, if not more, than they are his. You have the right to discipline them."

Emma sighs, probably weary of explaining herself to me. "We didn't get married out of convenience, to take care of each other's kids. We were raising our own alone and doing fine. We got married because we love each other."

Maybe I shouldn't have paid Troy the visit when I had, in the frame of mind I was in, but I really don't regret anything I said to him. "I told Troy that you deserve more respect from his kids and *him*."

"You told him a lot of stuff," she says resentfully, implying that I've once again broken confidences.

"Someone needed to." I wish I would have long ago.

"You talk about him and the kids not respecting me, but neither do you."

I'm taken aback. "What?"

"If you respected me, you would have let me handle it. You thought you needed to stick up for me because I can't do it myself." The anger is gone, but the hurt isn't. She's too proud.

And I trampled on that pride. "Emma, that was not my intention at all. I was upset—"

"About Robbie."

That's just the half of it, but I can't use the behavior of others to excuse my own. "I'm sorry, Em. Really sorry."

"Troy says you're starting trouble with everybody because you're not happy and you don't want anyone else to be happy." She drags in a deep breath. "He says you're probably responsible for Pam leaving Keith."

That hurts. "You know I had nothing to do with that. I want Pam and Keith to get back together."

But it's not going to happen. Pam can't be happy with Keith, so why would I want them back together? Troy's just lashing out, like I did at him. But I can't argue that I'm happy.

"I know that, Holly." She sighs. "I told Troy he was full of shit." She takes a deep breath. "And I told him you were right."

"Em!"

"I told him things were going to change, or he could go back to his cheating ex-wife if that's the kind of woman he wants raising his kids."

"Good for you!"

"I stuck up for myself, Holly." Her voice is soft as she adds, "*You* didn't need to."

"I'm sorry," I say, but she's already turning away and heading toward the door.

I want to stop her, to ask her to share with me everything that Troy said and did. I want to know if he's going to start giving her the respect she deserves. But she's right, I have to respect her, too. We may be sisters, but there are lines that can't be crossed, privacies that can't be violated.

"I'm sorry," I say again, but she's already gone.

Loud knocking awakens me. I straighten up on the couch, groaning from the crick in my neck. I fell asleep sitting up, never a comfortable position, but certainly better than sharing a bed with Claire.

I glance at the clock. It hasn't been long since Emma left. I hope it's her coming back, but the fact that she would now knock gives me no hope of repairing the damage my visit to Troy has done to our relationship. I will do it, but probably not today. Since I didn't get much sleep, I don't have enough brain cells firing.

I fling the front door open to a man in uniform. I know I don't have enough brain cells firing to deal with *him* and nearly slam the door closed. He must see the intention on my face because he puts his foot just over the threshold, even though I haven't invited him inside.

"Deputy Westmoreland." My voice is cool enough to my ears to make me shiver.

He smiles. "Call me Nathan. I'm not here in an official capacity."

"Not this time."

"Hopefully not again." But his tone reveals his doubt. He doesn't think I can keep my kids out of trouble without his help.

Once again I will tell him I don't need it. That I can raise my children by myself. Is lying to a police officer a crime?

"So why are you here?" I ask, even though I know the answer. I'm looking for the opportunity to tell him off. After my conversation with Emma and my lack of sleep, I'm looking for another cupcake to crush.

But Deputy Westmoreland—Nathan—with his wide shoulders and close-cropped black hair, is hardly a cupcake. I bet there is not one ounce of fat on him. He is big and hard and…

My face heats. I'm probably getting sick from lack of sleep.

"I wanted to check on Claire," he says, but I'm the one he's watching. Too closely. He looks about to reach out and touch my forehead, probably to see how high a fever I'm running.

It must be high because I shiver again. That could be because of the cool air swirling with dead leaves through the open door. I relent and step back, waving him in with a sweep of my arm.

He smiles as he walks past me. Although it's quite large, with a vaulted ceiling, the great room seems to shrink with his entrance. In that way, and only that way, he reminds me of Rob; rooms always shrank when Rob walked into them. I'd thought it was due to his booming voice and laugh. Deputy Westmoreland is quiet and serious, but his presence is somehow even more overwhelming.

I close the door behind him and lean against it. I'm so tired my knees are weak.

"So how is she?" he asks.

Claire. I'd almost forgotten the reason for his visit. "She's sleeping."

Or so I thought. Now that I'm awake, I can hear the murmur of the TV coming from my bedroom.

"Rough night?" he asks, again watching me too closely.

I run a hand through my disheveled hair, knowing that I probably look like hell. It shouldn't bother me that he would see me this way. He's seen me worse—hysterical. But for some reason it does bother me now.

"Yes," I admit.

Rough couple of days. I can't believe that's all it's been since the situation with my children has spiraled out of control.

"She was pretty upset at the house yesterday."

He'd been there with her before I'd remembered where I'd left my child and come to get her. No wonder he doesn't have much respect for my parenting skills. But still my pride stings, and I understand Emma's anger even more.

"I'm sure it has as much to do with her father as with Mrs. Diller," he adds with a commiserating sigh. "It opened all that pain up for her again."

I understand the grief counselor knowing that, but why does he?

"So they teach psychology at the police academy now?" I ask, knowing I sound bitchy. But then I probably always sound bitchy to him. I can't control the anger that wells up in me every time I have to deal with him.

He nods. "Yes, they do, but I took it in college, admittedly a while ago. I have a minor in it and a major in criminal justice." He sounds offended and irritated again, as if I treat him like he's an idiot. Obviously I piss him off as much as he does me. Why do we have this effect on each other?

As usual I don't waste time analyzing it, I just react. He may not look the part, but today he will be the cupcake.

"So that's why you think you can do a better job of helping my kids through this than I can?" I wince at my nastiness, but it doesn't stop me. "Because of your *minor* in psychology from *years* ago?"

I notice that his hair isn't entirely black—silver strands are woven in at his temples. But I'd already figured he was older than me.

"That's not why," he says.

"Oh, you just think I'm doing such a lousy job that anyone can do better?"

He steps closer now. Maybe he intends to leave,

but I'm blocking the door. "You are determined to take everything I do and say the wrong way."

"You make it easy for me to do that," I retort.

"Why is it so hard for you to believe that I want to help? That's what I do, you know." He taps the badge on his shirt, bringing my attention to his chest.

I focus on the badge, on his name and the series of numbers embossed in the shiny metal. "You work with teens *at risk*."

"I caught Robbie shoplifting," he reminds me.

"How? What, are you following him around, waiting for him to screw up?" I'm getting madder yet. "Isn't that police harassment? I could press charges."

He cups his big hand over my mouth, stemming the flow of angry words I was building up to. "Shh…"

I pry his hand away. "Don't shush me! I am not hysterical."

This time.

"So now you're going to accuse me of police brutality," he says. Something flashes through his green eyes, probably the temptation to brutalize me.

I'm glad I have not let go of his hand even though the contact with it is causing an electrical current to travel up my arm. Somehow our fingers have become entwined, but I don't pull away, and he doesn't back off.

There's this unbearable tension building with my angry words; I feel about to explode. I jerk my hand free of his and shove it against his chest. He's so strong, so solid that he doesn't even budge. Unlike me, so tired and mad that I'm shaking like the hula lamp when I kicked it across my bedroom. "Damn you—it's all *your* fault! You're to blame for my kids losing their father. And me losing my husband."

And my mind.

His brow furrows as he stares down at me. He catches my hand when I lift it to strike him again. "Holly..."

The anger leaves me in the ragged breath I sigh. "I didn't mean that," I say quickly, wishing I could take back the words. And my sanity.

He shakes his head. "I think you do. It's been seven months, and you're still mad at me."

How does he know exactly how many months? Maybe telling accident victims' families bad news is not as routine for him as I've thought.

"I really don't blame you." Now that I've said it, and heard how ridiculous it sounds, I realize I don't. Not anymore.

"Then what are you mad about?" he asks.

Why does he care? Because he does, I have to be honest with him. "I want to help my kids through this."

"It's been seven months," he says again. "You have, and you will. But I can help, too."

"Do *you* have kids?"

A muscle jumps in his jaw, indicating I touched a nerve. He just shakes his head.

"Then why do you think you can help?" I ask again. "Because of your badge or your psychology minor?"

"Because I've been through the same thing they have. My dad died, too." His fingers tighten on mine.

"So has mine—"

"But you were thirty."

Thirty-two. And how does he know this?

"I was fifteen." The exact same age as Robbie. No wonder he's been watching him so closely. "And my mom tried going it alone for a while. Like Robbie, I was really angry. I acted out a lot."

"How?" I ask.

He knows everything about me, but I know nothing about him. Until he told me, I hadn't known if he had kids. Or if he's ever been married. I'm not even sure how long he's lived in Stanville. Until this last year, I haven't had any interaction with the police, not for speeding or parking tickets, but I'm starting to think of Deputy Westmoreland as more than a public servant.

"I did a lot of stupid stuff," he admits, "worse than shoplifting. I'd probably be in jail if I hadn't gotten turned around."

"Who did the turning?" I hope his mother.

"My stepfather."

And my hope evaporates.

I pull my hand free of his, and he steps back. I want to ask how long his mother waited. Three weeks or seven months or somewhere in between?

But now I know too much about him and I don't want to learn any more. However, I do want him to know something about me. "I'm not going to be getting married anytime soon." Seeing as how I'm not planning on dating, maybe never.

"I know. That's why I thought I could help until…"

I meet someone. Even if I were ready to start dating, there's hardly a vast pool of eligible men in Stanville. Would he be in the small pool? I glance down to his hands, which are bare. But what does that really mean? There are plenty of men who don't wear wedding rings. My brother-in-law Troy can't or he might lose a finger on a car engine.

"I appreciate your offer to help," I say, meaning it now that I understand him. "But I don't think that's a good idea…."

"For you or the kids?" he asks. He's watching me closely again.

"The kids," I'm quick to say, but I'm thinking of myself, too, and the fact that this man makes me lose control just like Kitty Cupcakes. *They're* not good for me, so instinctively I know that *he* wouldn't be, either. "I don't want them getting attached to you."

It was different getting Keith involved with them;

he's family, even though he briefly forgot that on the deck the other night. And Keith's a banker, not a police officer. He doesn't put his life in danger every day. Maybe it's also that I will always think of Keith as a brother before a man. I can't say the same about Deputy Westmoreland. And I don't like that.

"Why not? I may not have been raised here, but I've lived in Stanville a long time. It's home. I'm not going anywhere. Even if you get involved with someone, I can stay a part of their lives. Be a mentor."

"As long as someone doesn't shoot you or run you over with a car." The thought of which has my heart lurching in my chest since his getting hurt is such a distinct possibility.

A few years ago that had happened on the freeway just outside of town. A policeman had stopped at an accident scene, another car hadn't, striking and killing the officer.

"Oh," Nathan says. Despite all the hostility I've subjected him to over the past several months, this is the first time he looks as if I really hurt him. "I understand."

Does he think that I doubt he can do his job, or protect himself? It isn't that at all. But no one can control fate. Sometimes bad things happen; I know this for a fact. And with his line of work, he's tempting fate more than most.

Before I can say anything else, he pulls open the door and leaves. Despite all the times I've wanted to hurt him the way I was hurting, I feel bad.

But if he wants to tempt fate, like Rob had, ignoring those chest pains to continue his Kitty Cupcake addiction, then I don't want him tempting *me*.

STAGE 12

"Why does she look like that?" Claire asks me in a loud whisper as we squeeze into one of the few open pews left in church.

"She's dead," Robbie answers, before I can. "That's how dead people look."

She elbows him. I'm not sure if it's on purpose or accidentally, as the church is so crowded we're nearly piled on top of each other.

"I don't mean *that*. I mean why is she dressed like that?"

I peer around people's heads to the front and the casket where Mrs. Diller is reclining in a pale lavender suit.

"She looks fine," I say. For an eighty-two-year-old dead woman.

I've never understood people saying how great someone looks when they're dead. I got a lot of those comments at Rob's funeral, along with, "He looks like he's just sleeping." Then someone would inevitably add, "And having a good dream."

I'm still convinced that the grin on his face had been over Pam losing the suit fight.

"But she never dressed like that," Claire is arguing. "She should be wearing that jean dress thingie she always wore."

I believe she means her jumper with the birdhouses embroidered on the front of it.

"And her floppy gardening hat. That's how Mrs. D always looked. Not like *that*."

Claire is clearly agitated, but at least she's not crying. Maybe her anger over the way Mrs. Diller is dressed is warding off the tears.

"And look at Mr. Diller all by himself," she says, with sympathy and not anger this time. The sympathy surprises me more than her anger did. Even before Rob died, she was fairly oblivious to the fact that other people live in her world. I *can* blame Rob for that; she was his spoiled little princess.

Bill Diller had had no one to have the suit fight with, and he sits alone in the front row, nearest the casket. Simon Van Otten sits a discreet row behind him. They've exchanged a handshake, nothing more. I find that sadder than the way Mrs. Diller is dressed.

"Yeah, why aren't they sitting together?" Robbie whispers. Clearly this generation knows about the real relationship between the fishing buddies.

"Appearances," I explain. "That's why she's dressed

like that. Some people think a person should be dressed up at their funeral."

"Like Aunt Pam," Robbie says with a snort. "She'll probably be wearing a wedding dress."

"That's the only way I'll get married again," Pam agrees as she squeezes in next to him. "Over my dead body."

Having gotten caught, he flushes bright red, then sputters, "Uh…Aunt Pam…"

Instead of being uptight and getting offended about what she overheard, Pam puts her arm around him. Maybe a little too tightly, judging how Robbie squirms, but still with affection.

I chuckle and expect Pam to shush me, but she doesn't even though the service is about to begin. Since her cruise, she's a different woman. A more relaxed, less judgmental one. Maybe she didn't leave Keith for another man, but I sometimes wonder if she found one on her trip.

"What are we talking about?" she asks.

"And the organ music." Claire continues her critique of the service with a disgusted sniff as the organist plays a particularly mournful hymn. "She wouldn't like that. She'd want me to play. She loved the song the DJ did at Dad's funeral. That's what I was learning how to play, what I was playing when she…"

Claire sniffles now and leans against me. All these months of the painful, resentful independence of adolescence is erased. She is my little girl again.

I put my arm around her. "It's okay, honey."

"Dad's funeral was cool," Robbie says, his eyes shining bright behind his glasses. "People are still talking about Dad's funeral."

It's true. Every day I worked at The Tearoom, someone made a comment about it, about his clothes, the DJ or the Hawaiian-theme buffet. Rob would love that people still smile when they think of his send-off, but most of all, that they think of him. Claire's fears are unfounded; she'll never forget her father.

"That's why Mrs. Diller is wearing a lavender dress and why they're playing hymns," I explain, "because *some* people don't like to be talked about."

And Robbie's sitting next to one of them.

Pam still has her arm around him, so her fingers tap my shoulder. "Hey, I'm right here."

"Better than talking about you behind your back," I point out. That's the great thing about sisters. Unlike with friends, diplomacy isn't always necessary. You can be blunt and get beyond it even when feelings get hurt. Because you're family, you have to. At least that's what I'm counting on where Emma's concerned.

She's not here today. None of her kids took classes from Mrs. Diller. And even though *she* did, her memories aren't as fond as mine and Pam's. She still harbors some resentment for Mrs. Diller pulling the hair on the top of her head to get her to sing high notes.

I attribute that incident to Mrs. Diller's zealousness and Emma's tone deafness. Emma should have forgotten about it. The fact that she hasn't makes me a little nervous about her forgiving me.

"I was wrong," Pam says, out of the blue. She rarely admits she's wrong. She definitely came back from that cruise another woman. "You were right to do Rob's funeral like you did." She squeezes Robbie's thin shoulders. "It was cool," she agrees with him. "In fact, your mom is pretty cool."

It's good that at least one of my sisters thinks so.

Robbie and Claire turn toward Pam, looking as if they're actually listening to her, when she continues, "Your mom didn't care that people were going to talk. She did what your dad wanted."

"That was cool," Robbie says, swiveling toward me with a smile. It's the first one he's given me in a while, but I don't feel that I truly deserve it.

We can't talk anymore because the service starts. The whole thing, from the minister's sermon to Bill Diller's stilted eulogy, is solemn. This is the kind of funeral that Rob hated; he'd told me so every time we attended one, and made me swear that I would never send him off this way.

I wasn't being cool or uncaring of what others

would think of his funeral, I just wanted him to like it. It was probably stage three, or is it four? Bargaining. If I gave him the send-off he wanted, maybe he wouldn't leave. I didn't get what I wanted, but he did.

A party for a funeral. People laughing. Good music. Good food.

At least Mrs. Diller gets the good food part. We're in The Tearoom now for the funeral luncheon. While most of the mourners are at the interim at the cemetery, the kids, Pam and I help Mom set things out.

I haven't been around the past few days, but she still has my salads on the menu and a few set out in bowls to serve for lunch. Along with them are slices of cake, cookies and pots of tea.

"This looks good, Grandma," Claire tells her, nodding in approval. "It's the only thing she really would have liked about today."

My mom, hands full of plates, manages to buzz Claire's cheek with a quick kiss. "I'm glad you think so, honey."

Then she turns toward me. "Holly, I couldn't remember how you make that chicken salad with the grapes or that fruit thing. I think I have all the ingredients. Do you mind?"

I shake my head and slip behind the counter and through the swinging doors to the kitchen. Pam follows me. "So what's up with you and Mom?"

"Nothing."

"That didn't look like nothing at your house a few nights ago," she says, picking a green grape off the counter to pop into her mouth. Her lips screw up. I assume it's because the grape's sour, not because she disapproves of anything.

"You thought it was about you," I remind her.

She smiles ruefully, no doubt remembering Mom's rebuke. Maybe that, as much as the cruise, has changed her.

"Are you and Mom okay," I ask, "now that she knows you filed?"

Pam shrugs as her smile dims. "It's not like Mom and I have ever seen eye to eye. But you and she…you've always been so close…until the other night. Something's happened between you."

"You're imagining things," I lie. I should be worried that it's getting so easy for me to do so.

Pam narrows her eyes, studying me carefully. "I don't think so…."

"Mom and I are fine," I claim, and hope I mean it. Not just because of the lying but because I miss the relationship I always had with my mother. I am irritated that she hasn't told Pam and Emma about Smiley yet. I don't want the responsibility of keeping her secret; I have more than enough responsibilities to handle on my own. A memory flits through my mind…of Deputy Westmoreland offering to help me. I shove it out.

"Then why haven't you been here this week?" Pam asks.

"I've been busy…with Claire. And you're back now. She doesn't need me."

Pam snorts, something else she wouldn't have done before her cruise. "I've accepted that you're better at working here than I am. Most of the customers have pointed that out to me. They miss you. You've brought something to this place, something it needed. Mom needs *you* here, not me."

"What will you do?"

She shrugs. "I don't know. I have a lot of stuff to sort out before I think about a career. Like where I'm going to live."

"You don't plan on living above The Tearoom the rest of your life?" I tease. I'm surprised she's lasted as long as she has, going from a spacious contemporary home to that cramped little apartment. Apparently I don't know my oldest sister as well as I thought I had.

She smiles. "It's not so bad. You should see what I did with the place. It's more than livable now."

I'd questioned the livability before, but Pam can't be too picky—apartments are scarce in Stanville. The newest development is the condo complex where my mom—and Smiley—live, and that's ten years old.

"I'll have to check the place out," I say. "But first I have to get these salads done." I concentrate on mixing everything together, and try ignoring Pam's scrutiny.

"Something's going on," she says, "something you're not telling me about." She has that singsong quality to her voice, that promise that whatever secret I'm keeping, she's going to pry it out of me.

Mom must be concerned about the same thing because she joins us in the kitchen. "Let me help you," she says. "People are arriving. We need to get these salads out there."

As we carry the bowls from the kitchen to where she's set up the buffet, I see Robbie and Deputy Westmoreland standing together. Robbie shakes the deputy's hand. He's wearing that same smile he gave me today, the one I hadn't seen for so long. Now twice in one day.

The addition of more food to the buffet table lures Robbie over. As he fills his plate, I casually, or so I hope, ask, "So what were you and Deputy Westmoreland talking about?" And shaking hands on? Did they make a pact to drive me crazy? It wouldn't take much effort from either of them to manage that.

His mouth is full but he doesn't wait to swallow before replying, "Nothing." He blushes, and I suspect it's not because he sprayed food all over.

"People don't shake on *nothing*," I point out.

His flush deepens. "Okay, I thanked him."

"For what?" Irritating his mother? It even irritates me that Westmoreland irritates me. I shouldn't notice the man at all.

Robbie lowers his voice. "For not arresting me."

I should thank Deputy Westmoreland for that, but it's safer, for both of us, if I stay away from him. And maybe Robbie not getting arrested has more to do with my mother's thing with Smiley than Deputy Westmoreland. Robbie was with me when we walked in on them that morning, after all. He should know.

I must be easy to read because Robbie says, "He could have...even without Smiley pressing charges. He did see me do it."

A laugh threatens, but I manage to restrain it to say, "Let that be a lesson to you. Every time you do something wrong, you get caught."

"I know," he says with a sigh, even though his dark eyes are amused. "I'm just not cut out to be a career criminal."

"That's a relief." And so is the way he's talking to me, without all the resentment.

"It was stupid, Mom," he admits, seriously now. "And it won't happen again. That's what we were shaking on—my promise to stay out of trouble."

He'll make that promise to Deputy Westmoreland, but not to me. We're not making all that much progress yet. At least *I'm* not. I turn toward where Deputy Westmoreland is standing on the other side of the room.

He's shaking more hands, but that doesn't affect me, not like his handshake with my son. I don't want him getting any more involved with my family. In all honesty, I don't want him getting any closer to them…or me. For a police officer, he must not be all that observant because he doesn't notice me staring at him.

Someone else does, though. Pam bumps my shoulder. "Are you thinking about breaking the law, little sister?"

"I don't need another lawbreaker in my house," I say, deliberately ignoring her not-so-subtle innuendo.

"I'm thinking about it," she admits, with a deep sigh, "just so he could slap the cuffs on me—"

"Pam!"

"Hey, I'm almost single. I can look," she says in self-defense.

"Keith's here," I point out, as I see him milling around in the group now filling The Tearoom to capacity or beyond. Isn't that some type of violation? But the deputy doesn't notice that, either.

Pam nods. "I'll talk to him in a minute."

So she's not done with me yet. My attention is drawn to the buffet table, to where the carrot cake is going fast. If she keeps me much longer, I won't get a piece. "What?" I ask her impatiently.

"*You* can look," she says.

Apparently I'm not as easy to read as I think because she's not talking about the carrot cake.

"You're already single," she adds.

Before I can set her straight, she's gone...and so is the last slice of carrot cake. I sigh. I guess I can make do with some salad. But those bowls are looking low. I start toward the kitchen, glancing back at Pam and Keith as I slip behind the counter. Their heads are close together, and they're both smiling.

I know not to hope for a reconciliation though because they don't even look like husband and wife anymore. They're talking like friends, which is a good thing. I worry about them losing that. They have a child together, will have grandchildren together someday; it's important that they can be more than just civil with each other.

Then I push through the swinging doors to the kitchen and have to remind *myself* to be civil. It's probably the most I can hope for with the way Westmoreland makes me lose it.

He's standing near the walk-in cooler, holding a plate. He hasn't touched the slice of cake on it; there are no fork marks in the cream cheese frosting. I think about opening the door, taking the plate and shoving him into the cooler, but he's much too big for me to manage that. Who am I kidding? He's just too much for me to manage.

I try to ignore him and concentrate on making more salad, but he's standing too close. He puts the plate in front of me. "I saved this for you."

"For me?" How did he know? Obviously he's far more observant than I thought.

"I know it's your favorite."

So he hasn't been watching me *just* today, but other times, as well, when I've been here and he's been here. Although I ignore him, or I try, he's apparently *not* ignoring me. A little shiver chases down my spine, and I glance to the cooler again, to make sure the door isn't open. But it's not a draft I'm feeling.

I can't admit what I'm feeling. To do so would be a betrayal, and there's already so much I feel guilty about.

"With your sister keeping you talking, you were going to miss out."

Even though he saved me a slice, I still feel as though I've missed out because now I have to put my hostility aside. "Thank you."

He smiles, a slow grin that lightens his dark gray-green eyes to sage. I hate that I notice that.

"You're pleased with yourself," I comment.

On principle, I shouldn't let the cake tempt me, but I've already picked up a fork and sliced off a piece. I skipped breakfast this morning. There had been a crisis over Claire having *nothing* to wear. It's funny how I was able to find many suitable things in her closet, though.

"I was hoping you'd accept the cake as a peace offering," he admits.

My mouth is too full for me to ask over what he's offering peace, but he answers me anyway. "I could tell you were ticked off that I talked to Robbie today."

Does the man have eyes in the back of his head? He's facing me now, so I can't check.

"He came up to me," Westmoreland explains.

I may be little, but obviously something about me intimidates him enough that he feels the need to defend himself. He's not the only one.

I lick frosting off the fork, then point the tines at him. "I specifically told you that I don't want you having anything to do with my kids," I remind him a bit too vehemently.

"It took a lot of guts for him to approach me," he says, with respect for my son, as he tries to reason with his unreasonable mother.

I nod, too choked up with pride to say more. Robbie is a good kid.

"I wasn't going to just walk away from him," Nathan explains.

"I really wish you would have," I say heavily. "I really wish you'd leave us alone." So that I don't have these thoughts about him, so that I don't keep noticing how broad his shoulders are, how big his arms and chest are. So that I don't wonder if his hugs might be as warm and comforting as Rob's.

Rob.

"Why can't you just leave us alone?" I ask, blinking back the tears beginning to pool in my eyes.

"Because I care too much."

My heart does a little skip in my chest, and I drop the fork to press my hand against it. He can't mean... about me. I've given him no encouragement, nothing but aggravation and hostility.

"I told you," he reminds me, "I can identify with Robbie. And I'm worried about him. It's not just Claire who's going to be affected by the first funeral since their dad's."

"No, it's not," I admit. But so far, the effects on Robbie have been good. Those smiles. That promise to stay out of trouble. Even if it wasn't made to me, it was made.

Deputy Westmoreland blows out a ragged breath. "I'm sorry." Suddenly his hand is on the side of my face, his wide palm cupping my cheek. "I didn't think about what you must be going through...."

Neither did I...until now. My breath grows shallow as my heart beats hard. Guilt and regret and so many other emotions roll over me so fast and so hard that I sway a bit on my heels.

"I'm fine," I say, but I sound weak and pathetic. I hate that. And I hate him for making me feel this way.

I bristle, intending to blast him for that when he says, "I know you loved your husband very much."

I *did*.

And all of a sudden Rob is past tense. My life has gone on without him. This is the first time I really realize that. My knees weaken.

"I need to sit down," I acknowledge, but there's no chair in the kitchen, just stainless steel appliances and counters.

Westmoreland's hand moves from my face to my waist, his other one joins it, and he lifts me onto the counter. The steel is cold beneath the thin material of my skirt and hose.

"Are you okay?" he asks with real concern. "Are you going to pass out?"

I assume all the color has drained from my face. I must look attractive.

"Put your head between your knees," he advises as his hand closes around the back of my neck.

I grab his arm. "I'm fine, really."

This time I mean it. My fingers clutch instead of release his arm, though.

"I skipped breakfast," I say, because the real reason I needed to sit down is too personal.

But then the deputy and I have gotten awfully personal lately. That needs to stop, but still I don't let him go. It feels good to touch someone, to touch *him*. "Don't worry about me."

I mean it. His concern for me makes me far more uncomfortable than his concern for my children.

"It was hard for my mom, too," he says quietly.

"What? Having a pain in the ass for a son?" I can't believe I said that last bit aloud, but it's due to my defensiveness now more than my usual loss of control around him.

Obviously he knows that because he ignores my comment. "She couldn't talk about my father, either."

I think about Rob all the time, but do I talk about him to the kids or just to the lamp?

"It made it harder for me. I felt like I couldn't mourn him because she wasn't mourning him."

"I mourn Rob." I hate this defensiveness, but I hate him more. And I hate myself for noticing a man other than my husband. It doesn't matter that Rob is dead; I'm still married. "How dare you suggest I haven't!"

"Do your kids know you have? Have they seen you cry?"

In those first few weeks, they saw me cry lots of times. "Sure."

"Lately or just in the beginning?"

He knows too much.

"I have to be strong for them," I remind him. "I have to move on, so they can move on."

"Why? Why do you have to move on?" he asks. "My mother got rid of everything of my father's. She took him away from me more than his dying did."

I'm struck by the eerie similarities.

"You do understand Robbie," I have to admit. More than I will ever be able to. I've never been a teenage boy without a father.

"I do." He smiles again, but his eyes don't lighten as much. "I wore glasses and was small for my age, too."

His arm is hard beneath my fingers. Even sitting on the counter as I am, he has to dip his head to meet my gaze. I find it difficult to believe he was ever small. I look into his eyes.

"No contacts." My observation comes out breathlessly, but I refuse to analyze why.

"Astigmatism. Outgrew it."

"Among other things," I say.

"Not my attitude. I had a bad one for a long time."

I smile. "I'm not so sure you outgrew that."

He sighs. "I know I'm pretty intense, but it's just that Robbie reminds me so much of me at his age."

"And you got in a lot of trouble?"

He nods. "God knows what would have happened to me if not for my stepfather." He sighs again. "I probably wouldn't be here. My mom has admitted she thought she was going to lose me, too."

I shiver again, having known that fear the night Robbie ran away and the night he came home in the back of a police cruiser. Even though Robbie has been better lately, I can't risk losing him.

I draw in a deep, fortifying breath, then say, "Okay."

"Okay what?"

"You can put him in your program." I have to do what's best for Robbie, not just myself. "Mentor him, whatever you want to do."

Westmoreland doesn't let out a rebel yell of triumph, doesn't betray any in a smile or a flicker of his eyes, either. As he admitted, he's intense.

"I'll be careful," he promises me.

I don't know if he means with Robbie or his own life, as I made the argument earlier that I didn't want my kids getting attached to a man in his profession.

"Just Robbie," I say, not that I don't want him to stay safe, too. "Not Claire."

She would be hurt too much if she loses anyone else she's come to care about. She's too fragile. And even though I'm sitting down now, after what I realized today, I'm feeling fragile, too.

I'm moving on from Rob, whether I'm ready or not. Knowing he probably would have already found someone else doesn't ease the guilt turning my stomach. I'm not like him. I'm not afraid to be alone. I'm more afraid to be with someone else.

STAGE 13

"I can't tell you how much I appreciate this," Bill Diller says, as he watches me pack up a box of his mother's books. She had a volume on every flower and plant known to man. Gardening was really her passion.

But so were children. She saved everything Claire and her other students gave her over the years. Scrapbooks of each child's colored pictures. I put those in a separate pile in case he'd like to return them.

"She was a special lady," I tell him.

He sighs. "Yes, she was. I know I was lucky to have her so long, but still…"

His face flushes, probably with embarrassment and guilt. "I'm sorry, Holly."

Why? Because I didn't have Rob as long? That wasn't Bill's fault. Truthfully, it probably wasn't even Rob's.

"It's okay," I assure him. "And you'll be okay, too."

"Of course," he hastily agrees. "I'm a grown man. I loved my mother, but I really didn't *need* her anymore." Even as he says it, he blinks back tears.

I reach out to him, where he's sitting on a chair near the spot where I'm kneeling on the floor by the bookcases, and squeeze his hand. "I think we always need our mothers."

At least I know I need mine. And I'm hoping my children will always need me.

He smiles, too embarrassed to admit it. "She really loved books, didn't she?"

"She loved music. She loved her garden. She loved life," I say, thinking not many people enjoy life as much as Rob and Mrs. Diller did. I know the mayor doesn't. He's too worried about what other people will think if he does what makes him happy, just as Pam was.

"She loved you more than any of these things," I remind him.

He nods. "I know. I was very lucky to have her."

"Because she loved you so much, she would want you to be happy."

He might know where I'm heading with this because he stands up and walks across the room to the bay window. "I think I'll sell the house. I have my condo."

"It'll go fast, so think about it," I warn. "Decide if you really want to get rid of the place before you put it up for sale."

"I don't have my mother's green thumb. It would be a shame to let all those gardens, all her hard work, go to waste."

"Yes, it would," I agree. "I know who's a good gardener." So does Bill. The principal. They could live here—together—if either of them had the guts to go after what they really wanted.

"Holly?" He turns toward me, his eyes wide with both a question and the fear that I already know the answer.

"You know who I'm talking about," I say, confirming his suspicion.

Despite being a politician, Bill Diller is not particularly slick or quick on his feet. "Holly, you don't really know…if you're thinking…you're wrong…"

I shake my head. "No, you're wrong. You're wrong to deny your happiness because of what some people might think."

"Holly…"

I stand up, leaving the boxes on the floor. I know I'm leaving him with much more to clean up than that. "Your mother would want you to be happy, Mayor. If you can't think about yourself, think about that."

He stops me before I make it to the door. "Take this," he says, holding out Claire's scrapbook. "My mother would want her to have it."

I hope that means he'll honor the other things she'd want. But taking that step requires a lot of courage, maybe more than he has.

It takes some courage on my part to knock on Claire's door with the scrapbook under my arm. Mrs. Diller might have wanted her to have it, but I'm not sure Claire will. She might not want to be reminded of the old woman or the childish drawings Claire made for her once upon a time. And I don't want it winding up where the kitty posters did—in the trash. I've just about changed my mind about giving it to her when she opens the door.

"You didn't just walk in," she says, both incredulous and appreciative.

Note to self: maybe it's time to start respecting her privacy. After all, as she's told me a million times, she isn't a little girl anymore. So giving her the scrapbook is a bad idea.

"What's that?" she asks, before I can turn around and run away with it.

I draw in a quick breath, then tell her in a rush, "I was over at Mrs. Diller's, helping the mayor pack up some of her things, and we came across this. He thought she'd want you to have it, but you're probably not ready to look at it yet. I'll just put it away until later—"

"Mom!"

Her urgency stops me. "It's up to you," I say, resolving to treat her like a young adult instead of a fragile child. "It's a scrapbook of all the drawings you've given her over the years. Do you want to look at it?"

"Sure," she says, surprising me. Then she walks over to her unmade bed and sits on the edge of it.

I look around her room. Clothes and earrings are piled on her dresser, and there's no place to set the book.

"Bring it over here, please," she says, patting the spot beside her. "You can look at it with me."

Together we leaf through the pages. She laughs at her crude artwork while I admire the little stick figures and colorful flowers. Mostly flowers.

"She loved her gardens," Claire says, with a sad little sigh. "If Mr. Diller sells her house, I hope whoever buys it takes care of them."

"They're too beautiful to neglect," I agree, hoping the mayor won't let that happen.

"She was pretty old, huh?" she asks, too casually, as if it doesn't matter to her. So I know that it does.

My daughter is becoming less and less of a stranger to me. Again I choose to take off the kid gloves.

"She was already old when I had her for a music teacher in elementary school," I say.

Claire nods. "Yeah. I think that's why I didn't worry about losing her. The other people I lost died before they got that old."

She's too young to have lost the people she has, the people so important to her. She continues in that same too-old-for-twelve, fatalistic voice, "It's like that movie we used to watch where the really, really old guy thought God forgot him."

"Grumpy Old Men."

"Yeah, the second movie." She sighs, resigned. "I guess I forgot that he died in the end."

I put my arm around her and squeeze her shoulders. It's nice that she doesn't pull away, but she doesn't snuggle against me the way she did those first few days after Mrs. Diller died. "I'm sorry, honey…."

She doesn't say anything, just keeps looking at the picture we left the book open to—a bright drawing of sunflowers with smiley faces. It reminds me that she used to be such a bright, sunny little girl.

"Do you want me to take the book?" I ask. "I can wrap it in plastic and find a box for it."

Like the lamp.

She shakes her head. "No, I like looking at it."

Maybe the only way Claire can move on is by looking back.

I've had a couple of weeks to think about what the deputy said about how he thought his mother hadn't mourned his father. Except for helping Mr. Diller with his mother's things, I actually haven't thought about much else but our last conversation.

Robbie has been working with him after school. I'm not sure what they're doing, possibly some sports in the gym at the high school. Robbie has always hated sports, but when he comes home, he's smiling, so I'm not too worried about him overdoing it and having an asthma attack.

I'm still worried about Claire, though. With Mrs. Diller gone, she has no after-school activities now. She doesn't want me to find her another piano teacher, and she still isn't talking to any of her friends, although a couple of them have started calling again. I'm not a fan of the manipulating Heather, but I'd rather Claire spend time with her instead of so much alone in her room, looking at that book of pictures she'd drawn for Mrs. Diller.

I have to do something. I have to find some way to help them deal with the passing of their father.

I can't buy back the business. I don't even think they'd want me to—Robbie doesn't seem very interested in the computer anymore except as a means to do his homework. Claire simply isn't interested in anything.

I'll talk to Emma about getting the Beetle back from her daughter, once we're talking again. Since that day she walked out, we haven't said much to each other, even on the walks we routinely take with Pam. Emma and I both let her do all the talking. Predictably, Pam doesn't notice.

Truthfully, I've been avoiding mending fences with Emma since I'll have to admit she was right, which is never easy. I should have respected her and the fact that she can stand up for herself. I shouldn't have butted into her business, especially when I resented Deputy Westmoreland butting into mine. Or did I just resent him? I don't anymore…at least not completely. I only resent the way he makes me feel, or the fact that he makes me feel—I'm not sure which—and I don't have time to waste analyzing feelings I never intend to act on.

During Mrs. Diller's funeral, I remembered why Rob wanted to be sent off in the way he was. He didn't want his death mourned; he wanted his life celebrated.

I haven't been celebrating. In my defense it's been hard not having Rob's pranks and jokes to make me laugh. The only thing that has brought much of a smile to my face since his death is the lamp, that tacky fire hazard that I keep meaning to drop at Goodwill.

I've kept it in my closet all these months, hidden away on the top shelf, which I can barely reach. It was selfish of me. I see that now. My fingers are on the handle to the closet door when someone knocks on the bedroom one.

"Mom, I'm home!" Robbie calls out. "I asked Nathan to stay for dinner."

Not Deputy Westmoreland. *Nathan*. That bothers me. *He* still bothers me, maybe even more than before. I definitely don't want him included in the celebration I planned for my kids tonight. I abandon the closet to throw open my bedroom door, but Robbie has already started across the dining room.

"Hey, you don't invite someone without asking me first." I remind him of another of our rules, one that we never heartily enforced. Rob always figured the more the merrier.

Robbie turns around, looking surprised. "Don't worry," he says. "He wouldn't stay. Probably because *you* didn't ask him." I try to hide my relief but Robbie asks, "Why don't you like him?"

"I don't *not* like him," I say even as a little voice in my head chastises me for lying to my child. "I just don't know him very well." That's not exactly a lie. I don't know him very well. And I hate that I want to.

"That's why we should have him over for dinner," Robbie says with a smug smile. "So you can *get* to know him. It'd be better than having Uncle Keith over."

He hasn't been over since that night he kissed me on the deck. Despite not wanting it to cause awkwardness between us, it has. I should have made more of an effort to get beyond the incident, but I haven't been making enough effort in a lot of areas lately.

"You'd like Nathan if you got to know him," Robbie insists. "Can't you call and ask him to dinner tonight?"

His persistence makes me nervous, but he's right—we do need to have the officer over for dinner. It's the right thing to do. And it's about time I start doing the right things.

"Okay, but some other time," I agree. "Tonight it's

just the three of us." For the moment. Someone else will be joining us after dessert.

An hour later, Robbie pushes his dessert cup away. "Strawberry shortcake," he says as he licks the last bit of whipped cream from his bottom lip. "What's up, Mom?"

Claire looks up from where she's playing with hers. "Is something going on, Mom?"

She's nervous still and a bit clingy with me, like she was just after Mrs. Diller died. She won't return my hugs, but she stays close to me.

I've made their favorite dinner before, but they pick up on the fact that I've got something else planned. Smart kids. "We're celebrating tonight," I inform them.

"Celebrating what?"

I don't know how to tell them, so I decide to *show* them. "Wait right here. I'll bring out the guest of honor."

They haven't moved an inch from the dining table when I return seconds later with the box from my closet.

"What's that?" Robbie asks. Now *he's* nervous.

Claire just stares at the box, not saying anything. She probably thinks I brought the cat back. I don't answer. I'm not sure how to answer, so I just lift *her* out.

"What's that?" Robbie asks again, staring at the hula girl, smiling.

I swallow hard. This is going to be more difficult than I imagined. "You guys think I got rid of everything of your dad's. But I didn't."

"This was Dad's?" Robbie asks as he reaches out toward the lamp. With a fingertip, he sets her swaying back and forth.

"I never saw this before," Claire says. She's obviously skeptical and not nearly as enthralled as Robbie is. "It's weird."

"So was Dad," Robbie says with a chuckle. He touches a coconut and blushes.

"Ewww," Claire says.

"It was in his office," I explain.

"You didn't sell it with the business?" Robbie questions, with a trace of his old resentment.

I knew celebrating his life wasn't going to be easy, but it's what Rob wanted. I wasn't ready for that before. I'm ready now. "No. The guys I sold the business to gave it to me. Your father kept it in the back room. I banned it from the house a long time ago."

"Because it's ugly," Claire guesses.

"It's funny, but I don't think she's ugly anymore. Still a bit tacky, but I can live with tacky. If you can...."

"You're going to keep it?" Robbie asks, turning toward me with surprise.

I shrug, then confess, "I fully intended to give her to Goodwill, but—"

"Why couldn't you?" Claire asks, her small nose wrinkling. She's still clearly unimpressed.

"She reminds me too much of your father."

"Really?" she responds.

Robbie laughs. "Oh, yeah." He and I share a moment, a memory. "Claire's too young to remember when Dad dressed up like a hula girl for Halloween."

"You don't remember, Claire?" It hadn't occurred to me that she might not.

She stands up, ready to run for her room, no doubt. I understand why she's upset, but we're not purposely excluding her. I catch her hand before she can get away.

"Let me tell you about it," I say.

She looks at me, brow furrowed with confusion. "You'll talk about Dad?"

Oh, God, why didn't I do this before? Maybe they weren't as receptive as they are tonight. But I should have insisted. I'm not a grief counselor who has to respect their privacy and their pain. I'm their mother. I should have encouraged them to talk. They were right—I have taken their father away, and I didn't even realize I'd been doing it until Nathan told me.

"Go sit on the couch," I say.

"But the dishes…" It's her chore tonight, so I'm surprised she'd even bring it up.

"The dishes don't matter." I mean that, just as it wouldn't matter if she broke them all. I don't need them to remember Rob. I have his children and my memories. "Tonight we're going to have a family party."

Like Rob used to throw these goofy toga parties

where we'd all dress up in our favorite Disney or Looney Tunes sheets. He was invariably Sponge Bob—to go with his sponge belly, he always said—when he wore the sheets over his yellow sweatsuit.

"We're having a party?" Claire asks.

"Yeah, tonight we're finally going to stop moping around and feeling sorry for ourselves. That would only make your father mad. From now on we're going to celebrate his life and the fact that we're still alive." I'm through feeling guilty that I'm here and he isn't. I'm not trying to replace their father, either. Although I know they'd have more fun with him, that doesn't mean that they can't have any with me.

Their faces mirror each other's doubt, probably in my sanity. "Mom…"

"Robbie, bring the lamp to the couch. I'll go get some albums." The only pictures I have of Rob that show more than the top of his head as he ducked behind one of us, are old, from before he emphatically took over as photographer. "We took our honeymoon in Hawaii. That was the excuse he used for buying the lamp and wearing that costume."

Robbie makes a face as he clutches the lamp close. "I don't want to see honeymoon pictures."

I laugh. "They're not X-rated." Not that Rob hadn't tried to take some of those. "Go sit down while I get them."

We sit for hours, the three of us, with no elbowing or resentment as we pore over albums the way Claire and I had Mrs. Diller's scrapbook the other day. When the daylight fades away, Robbie plugs in the lamp instead of turning on the lights in the vaulted ceiling. I don't tell him to unplug her even though I watch carefully that the dented grass shade doesn't catch fire.

We talk for hours, about Rob, about the stories we each remember with our own twists. I show them my keepsakes from when I first started dating their father, all those ripped five-dollar bills.

"Why wouldn't you go out with him?" Claire asks, offended on her father's behalf.

How do I explain how overwhelming their father could be? "I don't know. I was young, too young to get serious. And I guess I knew that all it would take was one date and we'd be inseparable."

And that was exactly what had happened.

"You loved him a lot," she says, as if it's the first time she realizes it.

I nod, blinking tears from my eyes. "I still do."

"He was the coolest," Robbie says.

"Yeah, he was," I agree.

"Check out that picture." Robbie points to one in the album that's open across the coffee table in front of us, the glow from the lamp illuminating it.

"I can't believe he dressed like a hula girl," Claire

says staring at the image of her dad swaying his hips in a gaudy grass skirt. She looks at the lamp with an affectionate smile.

"I can do better than that," I say. Rob's costume, something else I wasn't quite able to part with, is in a box at the top of my closet. "I'll be right back."

They don't stop talking as I walk away. They're still sharing memories of their dad, memories of happy times. But more importantly, we're not sad as we're doing this. We're laughing. We can be content. *Without* Rob.

I know it's not enough, but it's a beginning, and unlike all the times I've thought that before, this time I know it's true.

The grass skirt is a bit flimsy, so I slip it on over my sweatpants. When I try on the coconut bra, it hangs in front of my sweatshirt, giving me four breasts instead of two.

"Ta-da!" I say as I walk into the great room, hoping to surprise the kids.

But I'm the one surprised because Claire and Robbie aren't alone. Deputy Westmoreland sits between them on the couch, where I sat only moments before. Instead of looking at the photos Claire is indicating, he's looking at me. And for a self-professed intense man, he's wearing a pretty big grin, and an amused twinkle sparkles in his green eyes. "Aloha," he says.

The kids look up and start laughing.

"Cute, Mom," Claire tells me, trying to control her giggling. "I think I remember now."

She was so little that I doubt it, but I won't deny her the memory; I've already done enough of that with both of them. I probably would still be doing that if Nathan hadn't talked to me in the kitchen at The Tearoom the other day. I've decided he's Nathan to me now, too. After all, he's just seen me dressed as a hula girl.

"I'm sorry," he says, his jaw tightening as he smothers his grin. He probably figures, and with good reason, that I'm going to be mad at him for intruding.

For some reason it doesn't feel as if that's what he's doing, though. He seems to belong here, in the midst of our family celebration.

Before I can tell him it's all right, Robbie's speaking. "He brought my backpack. I left it in his car." The lamplight reflects off his lenses, so I can't see his eyes as he quickly adds, "By accident."

And now I know that it wasn't. He wanted Nathan to come by. Just for dinner? Or does he have another reason?

"We just finished eating," I say. Hours ago. "Would you like something?"

"We had gorditas," Claire says. "My favorite."

Nathan stands, and like before, the great room shrinks. "No, thanks. I already ate."

"There's shortcake, too," Robbie says.

"That's his favorite. If he's willing to share, you should take him up on it," I advise.

Nathan shakes his head and nearly steps over Claire to head toward the door. "No, I can't stay."

He means it, though I'm not sure in what way. Is he on duty? He's wearing his uniform, and his police car sits in the driveway. But then he's always wearing his uniform. Does he have a life outside work? I learned more about him the past few weeks, but not nearly enough all of a sudden. As Robbie suggested, I do need to get to know him better. He's important to my son, and if I was ready, he could maybe be important to me.

"You're welcome to stay," I say, and I mean it. This time. He's given me good advice and I should thank him for it.

But he's already walking toward the door. Robbie stays sitting, but he's watching us, not looking at the album, as Claire is again.

"Thanks for bringing the backpack," he calls out, not moving from the couch.

I follow Nathan to the door, then step out and close it behind me. "Thank you," I say.

"I didn't notice the bag when I dropped him off earlier. It was partly under the seat, almost wedged there."

Yes, Robbie did it purposely. Nathan knows it, too.

"I wasn't talking about the backpack," I admit. I can feel my face heating and it has nothing to do with getting caught wearing a grass skirt and a coconut bra. "You were right about the kids, about—"

"It's okay," he says, but his back is to me as he heads toward his car. "It's easier to see what needs to be done when you're not so close to the situation."

From the way he's still walking toward his car, it seems he's anxious to get away.

"We're a situation?" I ask.

"I didn't mean it like that."

I know he didn't, but we're both so used to me giving him a hard time that I can't stop feeling defensive. "Sure, we're your little charity project, like your at-risk teens."

He turns around. I've followed him to his car and he's trapped between it and me.

"God, you're infuriating," he says through clenched teeth, like Robbie does when he's mad. But then his jaw eases, and the grin steals back over his face. "Even in a grass skirt."

I touch the coconuts. "Don't forget the bra...."

A car goes by, toots. I ignore it although I'm sure my face is bright red. Since only my house, Emma's and Keith's are on this road, some member of my family has now also seen me in this wild getup. It's too late for Halloween, so I can't pass it off as my costume.

"It's sexy," he says, looking at me with amusement.

I doubt a man like him could ever find me sexy. That's good, though, I tell myself, stepping back. I wouldn't want him to, and not just because of guilt over betraying Rob, but plain, old-fashioned fear.

"I should get back to the kids…."

"You're doing a good thing," he says, as I walk away. "I'm sorry I intruded."

I open my mouth to deny it, but he's already closing his door and starting the engine. It's probably best this way. Even though he's helping Robbie, Claire doesn't need to get attached, as well.

When I step back into the house, music is blaring from the stereo—it's luau music—and the kids have fashioned makeshift togas from their bedsheets. Claire's is tie-dyed in brilliant colors. Robbie's is navy-blue with glow-in-the-dark planets.

The kids are dancing, and I start swaying back and forth as I move my arms like rolling waves. The coconuts bounce around wildly. We laugh, like we haven't laughed since Rob was alive. My heart is lighter than it's been in months.

Later, when we've settled down, Robbie rocks the lamp one last time. "You're not giving her away, right?"

"No."

"I can keep her in my room," he offers, as if he's making a great sacrifice.

"I want her," Claire says, the harmony of the last several hours fractured as she's ready to fight again.

"We'll keep her right where she is," I say.

"In the middle of the living room?" Claire's a bit appalled.

I know why. The plastic lamp with its wig accent and grass shade and skirt is horribly tacky and not in keeping with the country-cottage feel of the rest of the house.

I cock my head as I stare at the lamp. "Yeah, we'll keep her where she is. She looks good there."

Robbie nods. "Yeah, she does."

I pat my coconuts, which are resting on my lap now. "And maybe I'll wear this the next time I drop you guys off at school."

"Tomorrow's Saturday," they remind me.

"There's five days next week."

Their groans echo behind them as they head off to bed, leaving me alone with the lamp and the Halloween costume. But I don't feel alone. I'm not living with strangers anymore. I finally reached my children.

There's a possibility I may lose them again. At their age there are no guarantees. Not when hormones and teenage rebellion are involved.

But I vow to be like Rob was when he pursued me— relentless. Just as he never gave up on me, I'll never give up on them.

My only problem is that I'll probably never give up on *him*, either, and the love that we shared. I've helped my children move on, and now I have to figure out how to move on myself.

STAGE 14

"So what's the deal?" Emma asks. "You put Mom up to doing Thanksgiving?"

Ever since she bought the old farmhouse from Mom, that particular holiday has been Emma's. Mom, due to the lack of square footage of her condo, stopped doing the holidays...until now.

"I had nothing to do with it," I reply, as we are getting stuff out of our cars in the parking lot of The Tearoom. I brought a salad. Emma pulls out cornbread muffins. "What did she tell you?"

I hope everything, but Emma's not upset enough for that to be the case. Yet. I'm pretty sure that I know the real reason Mom has decided to take back this holiday, though.

"She *said*—" Emma's tone reveals her skepticism "—it never occurred to her to have a family party here until the lunch for Mrs. Diller's funeral went so well."

"Then that must be it," I say, as I head toward the front door with my salad. If Mom wants to host

Thanksgiving so she can finally reveal her secret, that's her decision, not mine.

Robbie's holding the door open, but I'm afraid it's not because he's being a gentleman. "You better get in here quick," he says, confirming my fears. "Grandma needs help with Aunt Pam."

Emma shoots me a glance. "What's he mean by that?"

I shrug. She'll know soon enough. This is going to be interesting.

Troy and Jason fill the doorway behind Robbie. "Emma…" Troy doesn't say anything else, just looks to me, helplessly. He's worried about her, and I'm glad. He really does love her.

I pat first Robbie's head, then Troy's cheek, then tweak Jason's multipierced ear as I pass through the door. "It's going to be okay."

I'm lying. I don't have a clue how this is going to turn out. Mom grabs me the minute I step inside, sweeping me past Smiley and a bunch of strangers whom I assume are Smiley's family as she drags me into the kitchen.

"I need your help," she says, and I don't think she's talking about dinner.

Everything smells delicious. The mingled aromas of turkey and sage emanate from the oven. Pumpkin pie, heavy with cinnamon and nutmeg, tempts from the counter. My stomach growls. I just want to eat, but when Mom wanted to have the dinner, I knew it wasn't going to be that simple. Lately, nothing with my family is.

"Pam has locked herself upstairs. You have to talk to her."

"What about me?" Emma asks from the doorway. She drops the cornbread muffins onto a nearby counter. "Doesn't anyone want to talk to me?"

She sounds like Claire on a bad day. And like Claire on a bad day, she's capable of breaking my heart. I wince and turn toward Mom.

"You talk to Pam," she tells me again, as she takes Emma's hand in hers.

It's going to be intense. Both their discussion and mine. I hope no one lets the turkey burn. I follow the back steps up to Pam's apartment. The door at the top is locked, so I knock.

"Give me a minute," she says.

I know that's not going to be enough time for her to absorb this revelation. "Pam, let me in."

"No."

Mom probably gave up that I knew, probably even said I was okay with it. Because I let her think I'm okay with it. I'm actually not very sure if I am. That's not fair to her, though. She deserves to be happy, and it should give me hope that she can be with a man other than my father.

"You're pushing fifty, not fifteen," I remind Pam with as much tact as sisters ever use with each other.

The door rattles as she unlocks it. When it swings open, I step back. She might have reverted to the old Pam who was touchy about her age.

She waves me into the small apartment, which she has decorated well. Hardwood floors and woodwork are gleaming with warm stain and polish. Walls, once white, then dingy gray with age, are now soft palettes of pastels—creamy yellow and pale green.

"I love this place. It's definitely livable now. Nice work."

She ignores my compliment. "You should have warned me."

Yup, Mom gave me up. "She asked me not to tell you guys. She wanted to do it herself."

"But she didn't tell us. She blindsided us. Is Emma here yet?"

"Mom's talking to her now."

"She'll be diplomatic. Since the family's here Emma won't make a scene. She'll be polite. That's what Mom was counting on both of us doing."

I have a feeling only one of them will comply with Mom's wishes. "You don't care that Smiley's family knows you're throwing a fit?"

"Throwing a fit? I got the shock of my life. How am I supposed to react?"

"Like an adult who cares about her mother's feelings and wants her to be happy."

"Is she?"

I have to examine my own feelings and resentment and put all that aside. "Yes, she is. Apparently Smiley makes our mother—"

"Don't say it," Pam warns me, obviously expecting me to go for the obvious.

"Happy," I say.

"So I'll be happy for her," she insists, more to herself than to me. "The turkey smells great. I can't wait to eat." She pushes past me to head down the stairs. "Mom invited Keith, too," she comments offhandedly over her shoulder.

"So he's here." I haven't seen him since he kissed me. This should keep things interesting. Revealing that secret would really test the resolve of this new laid-back Pam. But I don't want to test her, not over something so stupid and inconsequential that it *never* really happened.

"No, he didn't come."

I restrain a sigh of relief. "Rachael cooking for him?"

"No, she's spending the day with Michael's family."

At least they're talking again. I know Rachael wouldn't talk to her mother for a while after she left, and then again after she filed.

Pam admits, "I'm not sure where Keith's spending the day. I think he's seeing someone."

He was. Me. Although I didn't realize that was what he considered our dinners. Dating. I don't shudder, even though I should. It used to be the thought of dating would inspire that reaction in me. Maybe it's Mom's inspiration, her having found love again, that has made the idea less abhorrent to me. I'd rather blame Mom than someone else; I've already blamed him for too much.

"How does that make you feel?" I ask.

"God, go to a grief counselor for a little bit and you're acting like a shrink."

I fake a German accent. "Subject refuses to answer the question. Believe she is suppressing something."

"The urge to kick your ass. You're my baby sister. I could still do it," she threatens.

Now I shudder or at least do a good job of feigning it. "You're scaring me, Pam. But as your baby sister, I'm not going to let up until you answer me."

She sighs. "Okay. It bothers me a little. Not that he's dating someone else. I'm not jealous. I'm just a little hurt that he's over me so quickly."

"But you're over him. You said you haven't loved him for years."

"That's true."

It's that dog in the manger thing. Pam doesn't want him, but she doesn't want him to be with anyone else, either.

She sighs again. "I'm being horribly selfish, aren't I?"

I put my arm around her shoulders and squeeze. "I hate to break it to you…"

She shakes her head. "I guess I have it coming."

"You're just human, honey."

"And here I thought I was something special," she says with a smile.

"I think you are."

"Your talk went better than ours," Emma says, as we join her in the kitchen.

"Are you okay?" I ask.

She nods. "Mom's bringing out the food. It's time to eat."

Despite how good everything is, none of us eats that much. It's too awkward, Smiley's family blending with ours. It alternates between dead silences and spats of nervous conversation.

"This is fun," Robbie says, but he doesn't mean it. "Why couldn't we have invited Nathan? Nobody would notice one more person."

I think he's wrong about that. I'm pretty positive everyone would notice if I brought a man along to Thanksgiving dinner.

"I'm sure he's spending the holiday with his family," I remind my son.

He shakes his head. "He wasn't going home. His family lives in Iowa, and he couldn't get flights in or out in time to get back for work tomorrow. I told you this."

I'm sure he did, but I hadn't really believed him then or now. It's kind of like how he "accidentally" left his backpack in the deputy's car.

"Robbie, I think Nathan would be happy he didn't come along today," I whisper to him.

He glances around at the unhappy faces at the tables my mother pulled together to make one. She's finding it's not as easy to accomplish that with people.

Smiley picks up a knife and starts carving the turkey. Across from me, Emma's face turns white; she looks as if he's carving her heart.

I know this is Dad's job, but he's been gone six years. Other people have taken over his duty. Troy. Keith. Rob.

Rob will never carve another turkey for me. He will never wrap another Christmas present, only to force me to open it before Christmas because he can't wait for my reaction. I miss him. And now with Smiley in Dad's place, I miss my father all over again, too.

Claire and Robbie are sitting on either side of me. I sat between them to prevent any elbowing, but also because I needed them close. I reach for their hands, needing to hold on to them and assure myself that they're still with me. I can't risk losing anyone else I care about.

"Do you want to start the prayer?" my mother asks, noticing our linked hands.

While my lips voice words of one prayer, my head is saying another: "Please, God, have mercy on us and let this dinner be over quickly."

I'd rather be at our awkward Thanksgiving dinner instead of here, sitting in the long, winding driveway of the deputy's secluded log home. Why did I give in to Robbie's nagging?

"I don't think he's home," I'm quick to say, as I leave the Tahoe running.

"Maybe he parked the cruiser in the garage," Robbie says, using the Tupperware dish of Thanksgiving leftovers to point toward the three-stall garage.

How like a man to have a garage bigger than his house. The cabin might be deceptive, though, looking smaller on the exterior than the interior. For some reason I want to get inside, to see if there are any woman's touches.

But that isn't any of my concern. "You can run up to the door," I tell Robbie, "and see if he's home."

"I want to go, too," Claire whines drowsily from the back seat.

"Go back to sleep," Robbie says. "I have to tell Mom something."

The brevity of his tone has my heart lurching. Has

he backslid on all the progress he's made? It's as if he wants to warn me about something.

"You can tell me anything," I claim, bracing myself.

"I don't care anymore that you sold Dad's business," he says, patting my hand with the one of his that isn't clutching the container my mother has filled with food.

I'd counseled myself to be patient, knowing how long it had taken my sisters and me to accept Mom selling the farm. I can't believe how much more understanding Robbie is. He's grown up so much this last year.

But before I can express my pride in him, he explains, "I want to be a cop now."

Good thing I braced myself.

"You guys, he's home!" Claire interjects, wide awake from her after-feast nap. "He's opening the door."

"Come on," Robbie says, hopping down from the Tahoe.

I'm too stunned to remember that I intended to stay in the vehicle and wait for them. Shutting off the engine, I follow my children to the front door, my knees trembling because of Robbie's new vocation, not because the deputy is standing there wearing only low-slung jeans and an open shirt. Now I know he doesn't wear his uniform all the time, at least not in the shower. His hair is damp, droplets dripping onto the shoulders of his chambray shirt.

"I wasn't expecting company," he says, fumbling with his buttons.

Does he already have company? Are we interrupting something? Along with his uniform, he's not wearing a smile, either. Nor is there any welcoming gleam in his green eyes.

"Since you wouldn't come to Thanksgiving dinner," Robbie begins, confirming my suspicion that he invited the deputy despite what I'd said, "we brought it to you."

Yes, Robbie is getting too attached to the deputy, from wanting to spend too much time with him to wanting to be just like him. From the way Claire's staring at him, I suspect she could easily get attached, too.

But it's the look on Nathan's face that concerns me most, the mixture of pride and affection as he finally offers a smile—to my son. There are too many attachments forming all around. I have to put a stop to this…for all our sakes. Or someone's going to get hurt. And we've already had enough pain to last a lifetime.

"Come on, kids, we can't stay. I don't want your aunts waiting for me." They'll have too many questions.

There are some in Nathan's eyes as he meets my gaze. I just shake my head, silently indicating that we'll talk another time, without an audience.

He nods, understanding my silent communication in the same way that Rob had. I'd once thought the two men nothing alike. Until now. Now I know they're both capable of causing us pain.

Even if my sisters and I haven't managed our walk three nights every week, there's one day we never skip—Thanksgiving. After we gorge ourselves, we power walk off the calories. This afternoon we don't have to move that fast to wear off what little any of us has eaten.

I am determined to keep my mind off the slight detour I took between The Tearoom and home. My sisters don't need to know we stopped at Nathan's. Instead I'll talk about what's on all our minds.

"So dinner was fun," I say, and fake-cringe when they both hit my shoulders.

"You should have told us," Pam says.

"Hey, I was sworn to secrecy."

Emma snorts. "That's never stopped you before."

"I am not a tattletale." And I've finally proved it.

Pam blows out a breath, and probably not from the exertion of our power walk, which we're all used to. We're not used to seeing our mother with a man besides our father, though. "She says it's been going on a long time."

"You'd have to ask her."

"Holly, you need to tell us everything you know," Emma insists.

I lift my hands, palms up, in mock surrender. "I've been told to stay out of other people's lives."

She sighs. "I may have overreacted to your little conversation with my husband."

"I can't say you weren't justified. I shouldn't have yelled at Troy."

She shrugs. "He had it coming." Before I can gloat, she glares at me. "But *I* should have been the one to do the yelling, which I later did. We're finally, really blending our household. I can yell at his kids, too. And you're getting Rob's Beetle back. Troy's buying Sally a car of her own."

"That's great," both Pam and I say in unison.

Emma's smile widens. "Yeah, it is. And Jason's getting into that program with Robbie that Deputy Westmoreland runs."

If I have my way, Robbie will be getting out of it, so he'll forget all about becoming a cop. But I don't want to talk about that right now. I don't want to ever talk about Westmoreland—he's no longer Nathan for me— with my sisters. I can't risk thinking of him as anything other than the deputy, or at all.

Emma links her arm through mine. "I'm happy, Holly. Are you?"

There have been too many secrets lately for me to keep from them, not withstanding my little detour. I answer them as honestly as I can. "I'm getting there."

Having that hula lamp on the coffee table was a great first step. She makes me smile every time I see her. The kids are freer with their smiles, too—now. What will Robbie do when I break off his mentorship with Nathan? Dare I do that?

Pam, as always oblivious to anything not concerning her, says, "I wonder who Keith's seeing…."

Emma and I both laugh, although hers isn't nervous like mine—I never told her about the kiss. Does Pam have any idea what happened that night on my deck? I've just repaired one relationship with a sister; I don't want to have to work on another. There's enough on my plate already, and Thanksgiving leftovers it ain't.

"We weren't talking about you, Pam," Emma clues her in.

Pam shrugs. "I'm not, either. I'm talking about Keith. It's more interesting than Holly's on-again, off-again happiness."

"Thanks," I say.

"Oh, am I supposed to feel sorry for the poor widow?" she asks.

Emma gasps, but I know Pam's teasing. Since Rob died, I got sympathy from my sisters but never pity. They always know what I need.

"I hope Keith has better taste this time," I say. "He deserves someone nice."

Pam laughs. "I love you, too."

"Am I wrong?"

Her amusement fades into seriousness. "No, Keith does deserve someone nice, someone who really loves him."

"We all deserve that," Emma says, with the smug confidence of a woman who knows she's really loved. I've realized that she let Troy and his kids take her for granted because she was so scared of losing them, of failing at love a second time. But now that she's tested that love, by finally getting mad at him, she knows it's strong. "You need to start dating, Holly," she continues. Just as Rob played matchmaker for her, she wants everyone else to be as happy as she is.

"Not this again," I groan. "What's it going to take to convince you that I'm not interested?" I'd had a few doubts myself...for a while. The detour obliterated those.

Emma giggles. "It's a shame you don't live across the street from her anymore, Pam. You missed quite a show a couple weeks ago."

And now I know which of my relatives tooted a horn when I was outside wearing Rob's old costume. I groan again.

"What?" Pam asks, eager for gossip about *me*.

"Miss Merry Widow was doing a hula in her driveway for the fine deputy," Emma says.

Pam gasps. "No way! Em, were you drinking when you saw this?"

I'm relieved the story is too far-fetched to be believed.

"No," Emma claims, "she was in a grass skirt and coconut bra, had the deputy backed against his car. He looked scared, very scared."

If he was scared then, he'll be terrified when we have that little talk we silently promised each other.

STAGE 15

"**I**'m surprised you're this upset about it," my mother says as she pours two cups of herbal tea—one for each of us—from the pot on the counter between us.

It's Groucho again, his bushy ceramic brows lifted. I always thought Mom favored the pot because it reminded her of Rob. Now I wonder if it's because it reminds her of Smiley, with his bushy white brows.

Not that she needs any reminders of Smiley. He's usually in here, but this is a rare afternoon when The Tearoom is empty but for a couple customers in a corner booth.

"He's only fifteen," Mom reminds me. "He'll change his mind twenty more times before he finishes high school."

I want to believe her.

She continues, "Until just a little while ago, he wanted to be a computer guy like his dad."

"I wish he'd go back to that."

"Why?"

"It's safer."

"For which one of you?"

I'm not too proud to admit the truth. "Probably me. I won't have a heart attack worrying about him."

"Is it just him you're worrying about?"

"I already admitted—"

"I'm not talking about *you* now."

I feel like Pam for a moment, as if I think everything's about me. But it's not. This is about someone else. I know it…even though I don't want to admit it. Not to my mother, but most especially not to myself.

"So who are we talking about?" I ask as I stare into my cup.

"You know who," she says. I know she's watching me, but I don't look up. I just keep staring into the cup.

"Maybe we should get someone in here who reads tea leaves," I suggest.

She chuckles. "Might work…if I used loose leaves to make the tea." But she doesn't. "I'm not that old-fashioned."

That's certainly true. There's nothing old-fashioned about my mother, a woman who's been having a secret affair for years. She's pretty savvy to have pulled that off in this town.

"And anyway," she continues, "I don't think anyone can really predict the future."

"I suppose not…"

"For example, who would have figured Thanksgiving dinner would go so well?"

"Not me." I still don't figure it.

"You know, the turkey was moist. The stuffing had just the right mix of spices. And the pumpkin pie…"

"Fabulous," I agree.

"And the dinner conversation?" she asks. I look at her now; her blue eyes twinkle.

"Scintillating," I say.

She nods. "It could have been worse."

It certainly could have.

"Everyone behaved like adults." I remember Pam's fit and add, "Eventually."

Mom nods again. "I thought it would be worse. That's why I put off telling everybody for so long. Then the longer I waited, the worse I knew it would be. I guess I got into that habit after your father died."

"What habit?" I ask.

"Expecting the worse." She reaches across the counter and covers my hand with hers.

I study the blue veins, those running under her skin and mine. Our hands are so similar, like so much of our lives. I fear her habit is one I've picked up from her widow guidebook. "Is that what I'm doing?"

"I think so, honey." She pats my hand.

"I didn't used to be such a negative person," I say in

my defense. Happiness is going to be a little tough to maintain with such an attitude.

"You're not."

I lift a brow, and she laughs.

"Really, you're not," she says. "You can't help but expect the worst once the worst has happened to you."

She would know.

"So what do you do?"

Take up with the grocery store owner within weeks of burying your husband? It's too late for me to do that. Months, not weeks, have passed, and Smiley's already taken.

My mother shrugs. "I know you've been looking to me for guidance ever since Rob died, Holly. But the truth is you have far more answers than I do."

I shake my head. "No, I don't. I certainly don't know what to tell my son about his new vocation."

"Tell him you're proud of him for making such a noble decision."

I sigh. "I guess it was the logical decision for him when he realized he wouldn't make it as a career criminal. And it's less dangerous than that."

"There are no guarantees about the safety of any profession. Rob worked with computers. Your father was a farmer."

"Well, it was Rob's eating habits, not his job, that killed him."

"What about your father? He was perfectly healthy. He took care of himself."

And everyone else, in his quiet, loving way.

"There was no predicting the aneurism that killed him," my mother points out, tapping the rim of my teacup. "There's no predicting what's going to happen in life except for one thing…."

I wait for it, but when she doesn't finish her pronouncement after a while, I ask, "What?"

"Death."

"Well, that's not expecting the worst at all."

She shrugs. "I admitted I still do, even though Thanksgiving did go better than I expected."

"Okay…"

With that firmly in mind, I guess my happiness will remain elusive.

"Come on, Holly. I've been where you are. Your father's death affected me in so many ways. I got rid of the farm because I couldn't bear to be there without him. I got this place because I realized how short life is, and that if you want something, you have to go after it."

Rob's death had made Pam realize that. Why haven't I? Why haven't I gone after what I want? Maybe because I won't *admit* to what I want.

"What your father's death made me realize most is my own mortality," she confesses. "I'm going to die someday, too. And when I do, I don't want to go out of this world with a bunch of regrets."

"I haven't done anything I regret," I say. Selling the business, having more time for my kids…those were the right things to do.

"It's not what you've done that you'll regret. It's what you *haven't*."

I know she's right, but I can't admit it. I can't admit anything, not even to myself. She must know what I'm thinking when I ask, "When you first got involved with Smiley, didn't you feel like you were cheating on Dad?"

She bites her lip as she nods. "Sometimes I still do. When I'm thinking about your father, though, I remember how much he loved me. He'd want me to be happy, don't you think?"

I stand up and squeeze her shoulder. "Yes, I do. Thanks for talking to me, Mom…about Robbie."

She smiles. "We weren't talking about *Robbie*."

"This place is dead," I say, heavy on the irony. "Pam's in the back if you need help. I'm going to take off early."

She nods, knowing I need time to absorb everything we discussed. I just hope I *can* absorb it all.

As I walk out of The Tearoom, I meet Smiley on the sidewalk on his way in. For a moment, we look away quickly. Then I suck it up and say, "I never told you what I meant to when I came by that day."

He meets my gaze, wary, as if bracing himself for an attack. He just about flinches when I reach up and…kiss his cheek.

"Thank you," I tell him.

His fingers brush across his cheek. "For what?"

"I was going to thank you for not pressing charges against my son…or me."

"Holly, I never considered it," he says.

I believe him. I don't think it has as much to do with his relationship with my mother as the fact that he's just a good guy.

"Thank you, anyway," I say. Then I add, "Now I want to thank you for making my mother happy again." As Dad would have said, "You're a good egg."

He smiles, and when dimples pierce his cheeks and his entire face lights up, I understand how he came by his nickname. "I really care about your mother."

I know he does.

"Do me a favor?" I ask.

He nods, probably expecting me to threaten him to never hurt her. I already know he won't. "Start stocking Kitty Cupcakes again."

As my mother said, life is too short for regrets. I don't want to regret never eating another one of those killer cakes. I know now why Rob couldn't deprive himself of the sinful little sweets.

And I don't blame him anymore for dying. Mom

was right—there is no predicting death. I can't stop living because I'm scared of what might happen. I need to truly move on and go after what I want and whom I want.

I surprise myself when I pull into his driveway, even though I've known my destination since I left The Tearoom. A part of me might have known since the day Rob died I'd end up here but I can't think that, since I'm betraying him enough as it is. Or am I? Rob loved me at least as much as Dad loved Mom. He would want to see me happy, too.

In fact, Rob would be mad I mourned him as long as I did. He'd want me to celebrate not just his life, but mine, too. That thought gets me to open the Tahoe door and step down. Replaying Mom's little speech about regretting the things you haven't done gets me walking to his front door.

Knocking. Knocking is a whole other matter. And the only thing doing it right now is my heart against my ribs. This is crazy. This isn't me.

But then I'm not the me I was before Rob died. I'm different. Stronger. More resilient. I know now that I can handle the worst and survive. I can more than survive. I can be happy again. I can do that alone, like Pam, or I can do that with someone, like Mom and Emma, who both found an enduring second love.

But *he* can't do anything unless I knock. I'm making a shaky fist when the door opens.

"I saw you drive up," he says.

"I'm not sure why I'm here," I lie. I might as well; I've been lying to myself for so long.

"Well, I've been expecting you," he says, stepping back and gesturing for me to enter.

"You have?" I shouldn't be surprised. I already know he misses nothing. Then I remember our silent communication a few days ago. Of course he's been expecting me, and probably dreading every minute of another visit with the crazy woman.

"I didn't figure you'd wait this long before letting me have it," he says, confirming my suspicion.

"I wanted to wait until I'd calmed down," I admit— that was my reason for not storming over after the kids went to bed Thanksgiving night. I didn't want to lose control around him again. I was scared of what I might do. Now I'm scared of what I want to do.

"So have you?"

I clench my fingers to still their trembling. I don't answer him yet, looking around his living room instead. On Thanksgiving I was too blindsided by Robbie's declaration to notice anything about the house, but today I check for a woman's touch. The space is wide-open, living room flowing into kitchen and eating area. Logs comprise the exterior walls, but many windows brighten the room. The furniture is heavy, all the colors shades of browns.

"You're not married," I say, the comment slipping out unintentionally.

He narrows his eyes and answers me slowly. "No."

If he was, I figure someone would have mentioned it, since Pam and Mom have been aware of my interest in him, even before I was. "You know everything about me," I muse aloud, "and I know so little about you."

"I have been married," he admits.

I'm not surprised since he's too old not to have some history. "Does she still live in Stanville?"

"She never did." His green eyes harden. "She said she'd move here, that we would finally start our family. But in the end, it was easier for her to leave me than the city."

"Did she have a problem with your job?" Because I can totally identify with that. Even now, thinking of the danger he could face has my heart beating faster. Or is that because he's stepped closer and is staring at me so intensely?

"No," he says. "She knew it wasn't really any more dangerous than being a truck driver or a school-teacher." He pauses, watching me. "You don't have to worry about Robbie."

"I'm not," I declare. At least not now. "He's only fif-teen." Sixteen in a month, but I refuse to think about him coming of driving age. "He'll change his mind."

"I was just sixteen when I decided to become a cop," Nathan says quietly.

Although I've been in denial awhile, I've been noticing things about him, too. Such as when he talks quietly, what he's saying is very important.

"That's young," I reply, hoping to get him to share more about his life, about himself.

"It wasn't just a career choice."

I nod, knowing that, by hoping my son doesn't emulate him, I've offended him. I don't want to do that anymore. "It's more than that to you," I realize.

"It makes me who I am," he says. "I don't do it for excitement. If I did, I'd be working in Detroit or Chicago. To me, it's not about car chases and gun-fights."

Again my heart races as I imagine him involved in either of those situations.

"It's about helping people. Catching kids before they become career criminals, and working with them, making a difference," he explains, with more passion than I've ever heard anyone speak about anything.

If he's talked about the job this way with my son, it's no wonder Robbie is drawn to the idea. But he's drawn to video games, too, until they get old. He'll change his mind, but if he doesn't, I'll deal with my fears, even though the thought of my baby being in danger makes me sick.

"Robbie's not glamorizing it," he says. When I skeptically lift a brow, a grin spreads across Nathan's face. "Much. He knows it's quiet most of the time."

Until something happens. And you can never be sure when something will happen. In the past few months, though, I've come to realize you can't live your life in fear that it might, because that's not living.

I haven't been living since Rob died.

"Holly?" Nathan calls my name even though we stand only a couple of feet apart, and he has all of my attention. Then he reaches out, sliding his fingertips across my cheek.

I stare up at him, totally focused on his face. His features are a little too rugged for pretty-boy handsome, with his square jaw and deep-set eyes. His nose is a bit crooked and has probably been broken before, undoubtedly in his misspent youth, when he was acting out after his father's death. He's come a long way since then, from the angry young man he must have been to this caring, strong man he is now.

"Are you all right?" he asks, his deep voice vibrating with concern—and something else. It flares up in the depths of his green eyes, heating them.

No, I'm not all right. I'm scared, and I'm sick of being scared. He's a man worth being brave for, and it's past time that I find my courage to live again.

I slide my hands up his shoulders. They're so wide and

hard beneath my palms. Then I rise up on tiptoe, lifting my mouth to his. Now I'm scared that he'll pull back and believe I'm crazier than he's ever thought before.

But he doesn't move at all, doesn't even breathe until my mouth touches his. Then a sigh caresses my lips, carrying my name. "Holly...?"

He's silently asking a question, probably wondering if I've finally lost my mind. I guess he must not care, ultimately, because his arms close around me and he kisses me back, his mouth moving against mine.

Passion, so long dormant in my body, whips through me, heating my blood and my skin, and I know I could lose more than my mind, easily. My heart is beating so fast that it knocks against my breasts, which are flattened against his chest. We are pressed tightly together, our breaths mingling as our mouths slide hungrily across each other's.

His tongue slips between my lips, and I taste him, the lingering flavor of coffee, so rich and bitter. It's an intimate kiss, a kiss that could lead so quickly and easily...where I'm not ready to go.

I pull back, dragging air into my oxygen-deprived lungs. His chest is shaking a bit, too, as his breath comes raggedly. The green of his eyes is only a thin circle around his dilated pupils. He runs a slightly shaking hand through his disheveled hair. "I didn't think you even liked me...."

Despite all the emotions reeling through me, I smile. I'd thought he'd noticed everything about me, but still I managed to surprise him. He's not the only one. I blink hard, fighting back the moisture springing to my eyes.

"I think I like you too much," I admit, my voice breaking.

"And you're not ready," he says—as always, understanding.

That's why I like him too much. And why I've hated him, too. He gets under my skin too easily, too deeply, and I'm not ready for anyone to know me as well as he already does. Maybe even more than Rob did.

Rob...

Guilt slams through me, stealing away the composure I managed to regain. Despite the vaulted ceiling of the cabin, I feel confined, claustrophobic.

"I have to get out of here!" I'm pulling open the door on the Tahoe before he makes it to the porch. He stands there, staring after me as I drive away.

This—driving with tears blinding me—is more dangerous than anything he faces. His job has been just an excuse for me, a reason so that I wouldn't have to confront all these feelings that are crashing through me now.

I'm not nearly as brave as I want to be.

STAGE 16

Snow is falling, spreading a soft white blanket across the cemetery grass, as I walk toward Rob's grave. I haven't been here since the day we laid him in the ground, yet I know exactly where it is. I don't even have to look at the headstones. But now that I'm standing here, over the spot where his body lies, I can't look away from his marker.

As I study the words engraved in the polished granite, snowflakes hit it and melt, trickling down like tears. He didn't want anyone crying over him; I know that. But I can't stop—I haven't been able to since I left Nathan's house earlier today. I drove around awhile, probably recklessly, given my mental state, before coming here.

He's not here, not his soul. That's why I've never come before. Rob's in the daughter and son he left with me. He's even in that tacky hula girl lamp. I'm not here to be close to him; I'm here to finally let him go.

I can't move on with Nathan or anyone else until I do. But how do you say goodbye to someone who was the focus of your life for almost twenty years? How do you consign those twenty years to bittersweet memories?

If I knew how, I would have done it already. I thought I had the day we buried him in his wild Hawaiian shirt and Bermuda shorts. But that day was about carrying out his wishes and celebrating his life. His funeral wasn't goodbye.

I've been carrying him with me every day, trying to keep him alive. Rob would get a kick out of that, my dragging him around with me, like the characters had the body in *Weekend at Bernie's*.

I finally realized that today, when I kissed Nathan and felt like I was cheating. Not behind Rob's back, but right in front of his face.

Guilt drives more tears from my eyes. They leave cold streaks down my face, numbing my skin. I wish my heart were numb so that I didn't feel all this pain. But it's braver to let yourself feel pain than nothing at all.

I sink to my knees on the snow-covered grass, my purse slipping from my shoulder with my sudden movement. It's as if my knees folded, weakened by emotion. Along with my purse, I clutch a plastic bag of leis I found at Smiley's store. I bought a bunch of them a few days ago to use for another family party, but I'd forgotten and left them in the bag in the back of the Tahoe. Maybe that was Freudian, because I know now how they're meant to be used.

I lift out a yellow one first, Rob's favorite color, and drape it over a corner of his headstone. Its plastic flowers are a bit crushed and straggly looking, so I pick out another, an orange one, and drape it with the first. Then a blue.

Rob would like this, too. He'd make some crack about getting lei'd even after he died. As I think this, my hands shake, and I drape a purple with the others. Maybe he is here, because I can hear his laughter in my head again.

Of course he's here; I'm here. And I carry him with me everywhere.

"I can't do this anymore," I say, as I put the last of them, a red one, around the corner of his headstone. "I have to say goodbye."

This is harder than his funeral. That day I had my family around me, supporting me. I still had Rob because I wouldn't let him go.

Today I'm alone. Just me and the snow falling, the melting flakes dampening my hair and jacket. For December it's not that cold out, but I'm freezing. And shaking as sobs rack my body.

It gets dark earlier now. Day is already fading into night, the light eerily gray behind the falling snow. I need to do this; I need to leave him here.

"I will always love you, Rob…."

I lean over and slide my fingers along the engraving

of the single word below his name and the years that mark his birth and death. *Aloha*.

I pull my hand away and stand up, forcing my legs to hold me. "Aloha, Rob."

I turn and walk away, leaving him there, lying under those gaudy, plastic leis.

I notice two things when I walk through the door from the garage to the kitchen: my children are waiting impatiently for me, their faces tight with worry, and there are several boxes of Kitty Cupcakes piled on the counter.

"Mom, where were you?" Claire asks anxiously, as she rushes forward.

"It's not late," I say defensively, although I'm not sure why since I'm a little too old for a curfew.

"But you're always home when we get off the bus," she reminds me. That was my plan since I sold the business and work at home now. I even managed to when working for Mom at The Tearoom.

This is the first day I've not kept to the plan, that I've not made them the center of my new universe. Their concern should probably make me feel guilty, but instead it makes me feel good. It's only right, after all the worrying I've done over them, that they worry a little about me.

"I had something to do," I reply. But if I told them what, they'd probably hate me again.

"Nathan called," Robbie says, studying me intently. The more time he spends with that man, the more he acts like him. "He was worried about you."

And by checking up on me, he worried my children. Another reason I should *not* be attracted to the man. Even without Rob, I have so many. First, he just about arrests my son, then recruits him to a dangerous profession.

"He wanted to make sure you got home safely," Robbie continues, as if he's uncertain that I have even though I'm standing in front of him.

Claire's breath catches. "You've been crying, Mom," she notices, reaching a hand toward my face.

This time I'm the one to pull back. As hurt flickers through her dark eyes, I regret my action. It didn't bother me to worry my children a little, but I don't want to hurt them. "I was out in the snow," I explain. "My face just got wind-burned or a little frostbitten."

But my eyes are swollen, the skin so taut it feels as if my lids could burst. I haven't cried this hard or this long since Nathan first told me Rob had died. Yet another reason I should not like him, no matter how little any of it was his fault.

Claire shakes her head, then turns on her brother. I'm not sure if she's really angry at him or if it's in reaction to my rejection. "This is your fault!" she yells at him.

Instead of brushing off her accusation or fighting

back, Robbie draws in a shaky breath. Then he asks me, "Are you this upset that I want to be a cop?"

If I thought it would change his mind, I might let him believe I am. But that wouldn't be fair. "No. It's not about that."

Claire blinks hard, as if fighting back tears of her own. "Then what is it, Mom?" she asks.

I'm touched that they want to know, that they care that something has upset me, instead of trying to upset me themselves. I bite my lip, to stem a new flood of tears. I'm done crying. And I'm done denying my feelings. I blow out a ragged breath. "I wasn't doing as well as I thought I was," I admit.

"About Dad?" Claire asks, her voice breaking with her emotion.

I nod. "Yeah, it just hit me." They don't have to know why—that it was because I kissed another man. Although somehow I don't think they'd have as big a problem with that as I did. At least I don't think Robbie would—he idolizes Nathan too much.

"What hit you?" Robbie asks, as if he's ready to protect me, like his father had for so many years. His big, strong arms had held off all the fears and burdens that seem so insignificant now.

"It hit me," I say, my voice shaking, "that he's really gone."

A tear trickles down Claire's cheek. Although I

thought I'd shed them all, more fall from my eyes. I brush them away with my knuckles. "I really hate this," I say. "I want to be strong."

"You are strong, Mom," Claire says, her voice a bit awed.

Maybe I've been too strong. Maybe I should have shown my children that I need them as much as or more than they need me. I reach for her, pulling her into my arms, but I'm the one who cries on her shoulder now. Awkwardly she pats my back, then another hand joins hers. Robbie's.

"It's okay, Mom. You can cry." I hear the tears in his voice.

"God, I hate crying," I say as my nose burns and my eyes ache.

"Why? Because Dad wouldn't want you to cry?" Robbie asks, sucking up his own tears.

"No, because it makes me look horrible," I admit. "I'd rather get mad."

But I've done so much of that.

"Is that why you had Smiley drop off all these cupcakes? You were going to tromp on them?" Robbie asks. He tries for a chuckle, but it's strained.

I pull back from Claire's arms and take a box off the counter. No anger wells up inside of me; I can't summon any more. Maybe I've cried it all out. "No, I didn't ask Smiley to bring these."

But I have some idea why he has, as a bribe for acceptance in my mother's life. He didn't need to do that—I already have. "There's something a lot better we could do than crush them," I say, ripping open the box and tearing into a package. "Eat 'em."

"But, Mom, we haven't even had dinner yet," Claire says, appalled and sounding eerily similar to *me*.

I can barely restrain a smile. "Well, Robbie isn't the only one who gets to live dangerously." I break the cupcake in half and hold a piece out to her lips, tempting her.

"Mom," Robbie protests, "that's not why I want to do it."

"I know." And I do. He wants to be just like Nathan. This hero worship is something he might outgrow, given time and distance apart, which he won't get if I pursue a relationship with the man. Yet another reason to stay away from Deputy Westmoreland. Despite all these reasons, I know that I won't. Maybe I can't. Just as Rob couldn't deny himself Kitty Cupcakes.

Claire takes the bite I extended to her, sighing in ecstasy. Robbie and I join her, making a meal of the sweet treats.

We're going to be just fine.

Smiley had another reason for his cupcake bribe. I realize this when I surprise him in his back office and glimpse a jeweler's box among the papers atop his cluttered desk. He hastily shuffles some of the ledgers, but I pick up the box before he can bury it.

"Here," I say, holding it out to him, "you don't want to lose this."

He lifts one of those bushy white brows. "Are you sure?" he asks.

"You're not?"

He shakes his head, and the tufts of white hair standing straight up wave at me. Has frustration over paperwork or my mother caused him to pull his hair up like that?

I can solve one of his problems. I dressed in my smart little business suit to make a proposal myself. He's on his own with his…and my mother. "You won't know until you ask," I point out.

He sighs.

So I continue, "That's what brings me here. I was going to ask who was doing your bookkeeping and offer you a cheaper rate, but…"

What's cheaper than free? Not that I need the money. Keith's given me an update on the zeroes. He thinks that I, with my accounting background, should take a more active interest in the investments, but he's doing just fine. The kids will be able to attend whatever colleges they choose. I'm not sure what I want to use the money for beyond them, though. That's Rob's money. I need to make my own.

The couple of accounts I already have are a good start, but Smiley's would secure the success of my independent business. Before he can say anything, I add, "A good accountant can save you money by monitoring payroll and taxes and following up on outstanding accounts receivable. I am a good accountant, Smiley."

He smiles that smile that lights up his whole face and has dimples flashing in his cheeks. Once again I understand his attraction for my mother. He shuffles all the strewn papers into one messy pile. "It's all yours."

Too easy. Instead of elated, I'm deflated. "I don't want you doing this because of my mom."

"I won't lie that she's part of it," he admits, tapping the jeweler's box, "but not because I want to make points with her. It's because she's your biggest fan. She swears The Tearoom never would have made it if she'd had to do her own books. And with your help in the dining room, she's gotten even busier."

I nod. "Since I see her receipts, I have to agree. I've brought in more business. I can't promise you that I'll accomplish that for your store." I grin, remembering some of my thoughts about his inventory and some of the comments Pam made. "I have some ideas, though. If you'll let me bring in some help, I bet I can make some lucrative changes."

He draws in a quick breath, and I realize I've pushed him too hard too fast. He confirms this when he says, "My wife and I ran this store the same way for years. When she died, I felt like changing anything would somehow betray her. I knew I was wrong when I got involved with your mother, but by then I didn't know *how* to change anything. I've even thought about selling it. My kids have no interest in it. They'd never move back to Stanville...."

Buying the store? I hadn't thought about that. The Tearoom, yes, but the store is a major commitment. It would take more time and energy than I intend to give a career. I want a family life...and maybe, when I'm feeling braver, a private life.

"But I'm not ready yet," he says, chuckling. "I'm too young to retire."

From the lines in his face and the whiteness of his hair, he must be seventy, at least. But from the sharpness of his dark eyes, I agree that he's too young to retire. "That you are," I tell him heartily.

He smiles. "However, if I had someone I could trust keeping an eye on the books and stuff, I could spend some more time with a certain special lady. We could get out of this town, travel a bit."

"I think she might like that," I agree.

He picks up the jewelry box and pops it open. A marquis diamond shines brightly under the harsh fluorescent light of his cramped office. "Will she like this?"

I bite my lip as, for a moment, feelings crash through me. If, someday, a man offers me a ring again, how will I handle it? Will I remember Rob, as I do now, on his knees before me, needlessly begging for my hand in marriage? Or will I see only the man who loves me then and wants me to be his wife?

I don't know. I'm not prepared for that situation; I may never be. I just hope my mother is. So I can't answer Smiley. Instead I ask, "Why did you agree to keep your relationship secret for so long?"

"Your mother wasn't ready for anyone to know."

Somehow I think the person she most wanted it kept secret from—even though he was dead—already knew. My father. She's a stronger woman than I am to have been able to handle that guilt.

"That's why *she* kept it secret," I point out. "Why did *you*?"

The smile doesn't reach his eyes or precipitate dimples this time. "Because I love her."

"So you waited six years?"

He nods.

I am awed by the depth of his love. Rob loved me like that, not giving up on me, on us, until I agreed to date him. Will another man love me like that? Can I get as lucky as my mother is?

Because my mother's a smart woman, I feel confident in telling Smiley, "She'll like the ring." I'm not sure that she'll accept it, though. "Does our agreement hinge on your relationship?" I ask, all business. Making a success of something on my own, without Rob's or Mom's personalities being the driving forces, matters to me.

Smiley's eyes widen in surprise. "Not at all. If your mother turns me down flat, I still want your help with the business. In fact, I might be ready to sell it then and leave town."

I hope she accepts, so that I'm not forced to make a decision I'm unsure of yet. I'm going to have enough to handle with Smiley's account and the proposition I intend to make my mother. I know she's not yet ready to sell The Tearoom, but maybe she'll consider a partnership, letting me and my sisters buy in, if they're interested.

I extend my hand across Smiley's messy desk. "So we have a deal?"

His rough hand, callused from years of hard work, closes over mine. "We have a deal."

And I've just landed my first major client. Rob would be so proud. But he's not the man I want to tell. Rob's gone.

So is all my contact with Nathan. He hasn't called

me and I haven't called him since that passionate, emotional, messy kiss last week.

I don't think he's like Smiley. He's not waiting around for me to be ready.

STAGE 17

After the fiasco with the cat, I've learned my lesson about gift-giving to Claire. From now on, she's picking out her own presents. I haven't told her that, though. She thinks we're Christmas shopping for Robbie.

But I know how Claire shops for other people—in the stores she likes, picking out the things she wants. Usually.

That is not the case today. Today we've bought countless presents for Robbie. We have T-shirts, sweatshirts and sweatpants with every kind of police insignia on them, even some FBI. And now we're in a sporting goods store picking out a weight set for him.

"Weights? Really?" I ask her, as she lies back on the bench and lifts a barbell. She can probably lift more than her brother can.

"He really wants this, Mom," she says, and despite her track record of trying to irritate instead of please Robbie, I believe her. "He knows the only way to get over being so puny is to lift. That's what *Nathan* told him."

She says Nathan in a mocking singsong way. She and

I have heard his name too much lately—Robbie uses it to start just about every sentence. "Nathan says…"

Nathan says nothing to me. But then I haven't sought him out, either. I'm not sure if it's guilt, fear or embarrassment keeping me from contacting him now. I made such a fool of myself, running out of his house the way I had.

"Mom, are you okay?" Claire asks.

"Yeah, fine," I quickly assure her.

"You look like you're getting a fever. Your face is all red."

"It must be hot in here," I say, unzipping my jacket.

It has to be that because everybody knows a mom can't get sick. It isn't allowed. Moms have too much to do. Laundry, cooking, cleaning. Even when Rob was alive, he couldn't take over any of those jobs, not without shrinking my clothes, burning our dinner or breaking the vacuum cleaner. Now I suspect he did all that on purpose, so that he wouldn't ever have to fill in for me again. But he would buy me soup and flowers and press cold washcloths against my forehead when I was sick. I could use one now.

Claire huddles inside her fleece-lined coat and glances at me with a look of concern, probably that she might need to assume some of my jobs. "Mom, it's freezing in here. The place is a warehouse."

She's not wrong. When we first walked into the sporting goods store, I thought the place looked and felt like a meat locker. So if it's not hot and I'm not sick, it must be Nathan's fault that I'm flushed. And I'm not sure that it's just from embarrassment.

My body is reminding me that I need more in my life than my career and my children. I need to focus on me a bit.

Despite his questionable career choice, Robbie is doing fine. Better than fine, actually. Not only is he no longer skipping school, he's a model student—great grades and better citizenship.

Claire has lost some of her attitude, no doubt through the maturity gained from all she's endured. But she's still not completely herself, as evidenced by our Christmas shopping. Then again, when is a teenage girl ever really herself? When she hits her twenties, her thirties? I'm pushing forty and feeling as though I need to find myself again, the me I am without Rob, now that I've finally said goodbye. Like Claire, I'm making progress, but I feel as though I still have a way to go.

After loading the weight set into the back of the Tahoe, I've talked her into going to the mall. We're sitting in the food court, sipping peppermint-mocha lattes. Not long ago she would have refused to be seen in public hanging out with her mom. She would be with friends, and I would be far enough away that no one would know I was with her.

While I enjoy being with her, I miss those days when she had friends, when she cared about being cool. She doesn't care about all that much lately, probably because she doesn't dare. She's still afraid she's going to lose.

That's why it's so important to me that she gets what she wants this Christmas. I don't want her feeling like the kid on *A Christmas Story*, another of Rob's favorite movies, when he thinks he didn't get the BB gun he wanted. But she's been far more subtle than he was, because I don't know what she wants, which is why I have to get her to shop for herself.

"So you know how this works?" I ask, my tone teasing.

"What?" She shoots me a quick glance over the plastic lid of her coffee cup as she sips.

"Claire, I hate to be the one to break this to you," I say, as if I'm about to tell her something she doesn't already know, "but there really is no Santa Claus."

Her eyes widen in feigned shock, but then she snorts out a laugh. "I hate to break it to you, Mom, but I already knew that. I think I was six when Robbie told me."

I know, and it broke Rob's heart more than Claire's when she lost that belief. But it hadn't stopped him from dressing up like Santa Claus every year. He'd always joked that he had the body for it, didn't even need to stuff his pants with pillows for the bowlful of jelly, which had been a slight exaggeration.

Even though she stopped believing half her lifetime ago, this is the first year our family will truly be without the magic of Santa Claus. I push away the sadness. We'll make another kind of magic this year.

Claire must have picked up on my thoughts because she reaches across the small table and squeezes my hand. "It's okay, Mom. We'll be okay."

She's offering *me* reassurance? Like she had the night I came home from the cemetery. My heart swells with pride in my daughter's strength and compassion.

"I know you were thinking that this is our first Christmas without Dad," she says, making me aware that my daughter has Nathan's power of observation. I think *she* might make a fine police officer, but I'm not going to be the one to suggest it. If she comes to that conclusion on her own, though, I'll support her the way I'm supporting Robbie. As my mom suggested, I told him I was proud of him.

"It'll be hard," she continues, "but we'll get through it." She actually laughs, then shares her amusing thought. "It's going to be funny watching Robbie try to lift weights."

I refuse to give in to the laugh tickling my throat at the thought. Instead I say, "So we have all his presents. What about you, Claire?"

She shrugs.

"You know there's no Santa, no little elves making your gifts. I pick them out, and lately I haven't been so good at that." I grimace, thinking of the kitten debacle. "So instead of trying to surprise you, I want you to pick out what you want for Christmas."

I want my little girl to be happy.

She smiles and squeezes my hand again. "Don't worry, Mom." Is she reading my mind? "I'm sure I'll find something you can give me."

I wiggle my toes inside my shoes, preparing myself for a long trek around the mall. But before I can gear myself up, she asks, "Does Aunt Em still have my kitten?"

"Your kitten? You want it now?"

She bites her lip, then nods.

I know how much this is costing her. Daring to care about something again, daring to suffer the pain if she loses again. I am awed by my daughter's courage. And ashamed that I haven't been as brave.

"Well, if she doesn't have that one, I'm sure there are more." Emma really needs to get that slut fixed, but I'm so glad she hasn't. I reach for Claire's hand. She smiles, and her eyes are like mine, bright with unshed tears.

"You really won't care," she asks, "if it climbs the curtains or scratches the woodwork?"

I squeeze her hand. "As long as it makes you smile, I don't care."

"You know…I saw a pair of earrings in Icing that might make me smile, too," she says, tugging me up from my chair as she rises.

I groan, but I'm thrilled at the flash of my old, materialistic Claire. While we traipse around the mall, I catch a few more glimpses as she waves at some kids from school. But she doesn't shy away from me, pretending we're not together. Could it be that she's not exactly ashamed that I'm her mother? I'm proud as hell that she's my daughter.

"Close your eyes," Claire says as we step inside the back door. She takes the bags from my hands and drops them to the floor, uncaring of all the purchases we took so much time over.

I resist the urge to whine. All I want is to sink onto the couch and put my feet up next to the hula girl lamp on the coffee table. But that's not to be, as she tugs me past it and toward the stairs to the basement.

"I can't cover my eyes," I tell her, "I'll fall."

While she's strong, I doubt she's quite strong enough to catch me.

"Okay," she relents, "but you have to close them again when we get to the bottom."

An uneasy feeling steals over me. What have they done that they don't want me to see? Was this why she asked about the destruction of drapes and woodwork?

"Claire?" I don't ask more, I just squeeze my eyes tightly shut, uncertain if I'll be brave enough to open them when she tells me to.

I can hear a door open and a murmur of whispers. It's not just me and my children in my home. My uneasiness grows. I have no birthday coming up, no reason for them to throw me a surprise party. What have my kids done?

"Mom, you can open your eyes now." Robbie is the

one to issue the directive, as Claire continues to hold my hand.

I draw in a deep breath, causing a ripple of laughter among the audience to which I am blind. Then I open my eyes…to my children, my sisters and my mom. Standing in the background are the men: Troy, Keith, Smiley and Emma's boys. They're all watching me expectantly. At first I don't understand why…until I look past the people to the room in which they all stand. Rob's old den.

If not for the French doors opening into the family room, I might not recognize it. The fishing tackle wallpaper is gone, as is the dark wood and the heavy lodge-look furniture. Replacing them are deep red walls with crisp white trim and a white sectional desk and file cabinets. Robbie twirls a red leather chair toward me. "Have a seat, Mom, see if it fits."

The room swims for a minute, behind a sheen of tears, until I blink them away. "You all did this?" I ask.

"They did it," Pam says. "Robbie and Claire wanted to do this for you." Her tone is warning me just to appreciate it, not to freak out over what they've done.

But I can't help it. I'm stunned. "I…I don't understand."

"We're sick of eating at the counter because your stuff is spread all over the kitchen table," Robbie says, trying to joke, even as the tips of his ears are turning pink with embarrassment.

Claire slaps his shoulder. "That's not why. You're getting more work. Smiley's office is too grubby for you to work in." She flashes him a quick apologetic smile. "You needed your own space, Mom."

My space. Not Rob's. They turned his room into mine. I can't process the significance of this except that my children have made it through the toughest stage. Acceptance. They've said goodbye to their father, as I have.

"Do you like it?" Robbie asks, a bit anxiously. "It's your Christmas present from me and Claire."

I nod, my throat too choked with emotion. I notice the big red bow on the French doors. Like their father, they couldn't actually wait until Christmas to give me my present. But then they must have been working on this for a while, even with the help of the rest of the family.

Finally I manage to clear my throat and say, "It's beautiful."

"We had lots of help," Claire admits, hugging her grandmother and aunts. "Thank you. And the guys were the heavy lifters."

I, too, travel around the room offering hugs. I'm a bit surprised by Keith's presence, but Pam whispers that she invited him, then chastises me, "Don't get any ideas. We're friends. But he's seeing someone. A teller at the bank. And before you ask, she's very nice."

I don't have to thank Troy; Emma is doing that with a big kiss. Envy flashes through me and I admit I miss the passion of an intimate relationship. But I've already realized that and decided I need to do something to add more to my life than family and work. I need to play.

As I hug Smiley, I shoot a glance across the room, checking my mother's hand, which remains bare. "You didn't ask yet."

I have—not about Smiley's proposal, but my own. She's agreed to let me, Emma and Pam buy into The Tearoom, although she teased us a bit about how opposed we were to the idea of her opening it six years ago.

He shakes his head. "I did ask her."

My heart sinks. "She said no."

"No. She's thinking about it."

"Ah, Smiley…"

He offers his trademark grin. "I'm used to waiting for your mother, Holly."

That he is.

I hug her last. She clings. "You've done a good thing, Holly."

"I didn't do anything," I point out. "I didn't have a clue." This was the last present I would have expected my children to give me.

"You've helped your children through the worst tragedy they'll ever face. You're an incredible woman. I'm so proud you're my daughter."

I can't fend off the tears now. They streak heedlessly down my face, but I don't care. I shed more when I corral my children and hug them both tightly. All the people I care about are in this room, this special gift to me.

Except one. He's conspicuously missing from the heavy lifters.

I click off the cordless phone and sit back on the couch, staring at the hula lamp. She's smiling. So am I.

The first Christmas without Rob came and went. I won't say it was easy. The kids and I cried a lot, but we did it together. We also laughed a lot due to the new addition to our house, Claire's kitten. Taz entertained us by climbing the Christmas tree and knocking off ornaments.

A glass bulb falls to the carpet now as the tree shakes. Then a streak of orange darts from beneath it and scrambles, claws tearing, up the back of the suede couch. I wince, remembering why I didn't want a cat in the first place.

The kids are gone now. Rob's parents drove up from Indiana and spent Christmas Day with us. When they left, Claire and Robbie rode back down to spend a few extra days with them.

So I'm alone. Well, except for the lamp and the kitten, which has now shot across the couch, leaped onto the coffee table and is batting at the lamp. It fascinates the kitty more than it does us now.

As the kitten bats it, the hula girl sways back and forth, reminding me of my life lately, how it's ebbed back and forth between sadness and happiness. It also reminds me of Rob, how he never gave up. I told him to throw this away, but he kept it, like the cupcakes. He wasn't a quitter, or we never would have been together, never had those seventeen years of happiness, because I turned him down so many times before finally agreeing to go out with him.

From him, I have learned how to celebrate life, how to never give up. And from the lamp, I've learned how to sway with all the challenges thrown at me, but not break under the pressure.

I am strong. And brave.

I pour a little wine into my glass; another sits on the coffee table next to the lamp. I am alone at the moment, but don't expect to be for long.

Swirling the pale amber wine around, I take a sip, then lean back on the couch again. I don't need liquid courage; I have more than enough of my own. Finally.

The poor guy doesn't stand a chance. He hasn't been around lately, as he took some time off over the holidays to go home to Iowa. I only know this through Robbie.

There's a knock at my door, and I see Nathan through the window. I don't rush to let him in. For me, he's been inside for a while.

"Holly," he calls through the door, as he pounds again. "Is everything all right? Let me in!"

"It's not locked," I yell, as I pour his glass. He's next to me before the amber liquid nears the rim.

"What's going on?" he asks. "It sounded urgent when you called."

"It did?" I pretend to try to remember what I said, even though I'd rehearsed that brief sentence several times before I called. "I just said we needed to talk."

"'I need to talk to you *now*.'" He repeats my words verbatim, with the same emphasis I'd used. The man misses nothing. Did he miss me?

Due to the holidays and my new duties for Smiley, I've been too busy to spend much time at The Tearoom. That's about to change, though, since Mom and Smiley are off on a cruise to celebrate their engagement. His patience paid off with her acceptance of his proposal.

Has Nathan waited for me? I wasn't sure he cared enough...until he rushed right over at my call.

He glances toward the table and the wineglasses sitting there. "Do you have company?"

"I do now," I point out, handing the glass to him. "I assume you're not on duty."

He's wearing jeans and a dark green sweater under a leather jacket. I called his cell phone, so I wasn't sure where he'd be coming from...or if he'd come at all.

"Holly, what's going on?" he asks again. "When you called, I thought something might have happened with Robbie."

Is that the only reason he came? Because of his concern

and affection for my son? I shake my head. "Robbie's fine. He and Claire are in Indiana with Rob's parents."

Nathan nods. "I know."

Of course. There's nothing that happens in my house that he doesn't know. Thanks to his biggest fan. "I didn't ask you here to talk about Robbie," I admit. "Or Claire," I add quickly, so that he doesn't misunderstand again.

But then he didn't misunderstand anything. I deliberately misled him, unsure if he'd come otherwise. It's manipulation, pure and simple, but then so was Rob's ripping my tips in half all those years ago. And that had turned out very well.

Instead of asking me the obvious question—why I'd called him—Nathan takes a sip of wine. It's the dry, sour wine Keith turned me on to, but Nathan doesn't make a face. In fact he has no expression at all—his green eyes are guarded, his square jaw taut.

"I wanted to talk to you," I admit. "We haven't since that day…"

Half his mouth twists into a bitter smile. "You can't even say it."

"What? That I made a fool of myself?" I'd thought I was over that embarrassment, but my face heats up.

"That we kissed!" His eyes are suddenly hot, like my face, but not with embarrassment.

Anger, no doubt. We irritate each other so easily. Irritation and pride lift my chin. "I have no problem admitting that," I maintain.

"Then say it," he goads me.

I'd rather show him. I grab his jacket, gripping the leather in my fists as I rise up on my toes. Then I press my mouth to his. At first the kiss is hard and unyielding, how I once thought he was. But then his lips soften, and he's kissing me back. Hotly. Passionately.

We could take this further. We're alone in the house. Excitement ripples through me, quickening my pulse and stealing my breath. And with the excitement comes fear, like that in the pit of your stomach as you step on the roller coaster. Not the overwhelming kind that, mingled with guilt, had me tearing out of his house the last time we kissed. I'm scared, but I can do this. I'm ready. But I don't know if he is.

He pulls back and stares down at me with a dazed expression. "Holly…"

I smile, thrilled that once again I've surprised him. "Yes?"

"I don't understand." He's not too proud to admit it.

I blow out a breath, steadying myself for a confession. "Last time we kissed, I wasn't ready. I freaked out."

"I was worried about you, the way you left."

"But you never called."

He shakes his head. "I called Robbie, to see if you got home safely."

"You never called *me*." I try to keep the hurt and accusation from my voice, but it leaks out with the faintest whine.

He doesn't miss it. "I wanted to give you time. I didn't want to push you into something you weren't ready for."

"I did need time to think," I admit, thankful again for how much he understands me.

"I've done some thinking, too," he says, his voice heavy with emotion. "I knew your husband."

"You never told me…."

"Not well. Just from The Tearoom and the couple times I asked for his computer help. I don't think there's anyone in Stanville who didn't know your husband, Holly."

I smile. "True."

"He was such a fun, outgoing guy. He and I are nothing alike."

Tell me something I don't know. "So?" I ask. "I'm not looking for a replacement."

Nathan is staring at me now, silently. I know what he's thinking—that I'm still in love with Rob. Even though I said goodbye, Nathan's not wrong. He just doesn't know that my heart is big enough to love more than one man. I'm not sure yet that he's that other man, but I'd like to find out.

Finally he asks me, "What are you looking for?"

Not myself. I found her a while ago, kneeling in a cemetery beside my husband's grave. I found the strong, vital woman I once was, and no matter what happens, I'm not going to lose her again.

As for fun or happiness, I don't need someone else for that, not like I once needed Rob. I can make my own happiness; I know how to have fun, too. I wonder if Nathan does, though. Maybe he needs me for that; maybe he needs me more than I need him.

"Possibilities," I answer him. I've learned the hard way that there's no telling what the future holds. But there are possibilities. Nathan and I might be able to build a great relationship. Or, as we get to know each other better, we might irritate each other even more. But we won't know unless we try, unless we explore the possibilities.

His mouth kicks into that little grin again, and his green eyes shine. "I like that."

I think the kids will, too. Robbie loves Nathan already, and Claire thinks he's hot—her words. She is one perceptive young woman.

And even though he's gone, I think Rob would like Nathan, as well. He'd like the way he looks out for his kids, and the way he makes me feel.

Alive.

EPILOGUE

I've been through all the stages of grief, more times than I can count. But I like this last stage best, the one they don't tell you about. Happiness.

I've found it again. With my kids, who are doing great. With the career that's going strong now. With my family, each member of which has found her own happiness. And with the man who I'm now brave enough to love.

* * * * *

Who knew Truth or Dare could have such unexpected consequences...

Suburban Secrets

by Donna Birdsell

Opting for the Dare, Grace, who has let her Day-Timer rule her life, suddenly finds herself on an undercover assignment cooking for a Russian mob boss. Suddenly, her old life as a suburban soccer mom looks like heaven!

REQUEST YOUR FREE BOOKS!

2 FREE NOVELS TO INTRODUCE YOU TO OUR BRAND-NEW LINE!

There's the life you planned. And there's what comes next.

Stability is highly overrated....

Dana Logan's world had always revolved around her children. Now they're all grown up and don't seem to need anything she's able to give them. Struggling to find her new identity, Dana realizes that it's about time for her to get "off her rocker" and begin a new life!

Off Her Rocker

by Jennifer Archer

HARLEQUIN®
Next™

HN53

Available August 2006
TheNextNovel.com

There's got to be a mourning-after!

Saturday, September 22

1) Get a ~~dog~~ cat
2) Get a man
3) Get adventurous (go skinny-dipping)
4) Get a LIFE!

Jill Townsend is learning to step beyond the safe world she's always known to take the leap into Merry Widowhood.

The Merry Widow's Diary

by Susan Crosby

There's a first time for everything…

Aging rock-and-roller Zoe learned this the hard way…at thirty-nine, she was pregnant!

Leaving behind the temptations of L.A., she returns home to Louisiana to live with her sister. Despite their differences, they come to terms with their shared past and find that when the chips are down there is no better person to lean on than your sister.

Leaving L.A.

by

Rexanne Becnel

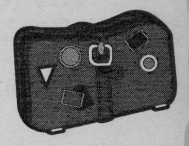

HARLEQUIN®

Next™

HN57
Available September 2006
TheNextNovel.com